# THE GYPSY TWIST

By the Same Author

*Spy the Movie* [Screenplay]
(with Charles Messina
&
Lynwood Shiva Sawyer)

# The Gypsy Twist

A Max Royster Mystery

by Frank Hickey

The Gypsy Twist: A Max Royster Mystery
Copyright © 2012 by Frank Hickey

All rights reserved. No part of this book may be reproduced or utilized in any form or by any means, mechanical or electronic, including manual re-input, photocopying, scanning, optical character recognition, recording or by any information storage and retrieval system without permission in writing from the copyright holder.

This novel is a work of fiction. All characters and events described herein are fictitious and wholly the product of the author's imagination. Any resemblance to actual persons, living or dead, is unintentional and coincidental.

Library of Congress
Catalogue-in-Publication Data

The Gypsy Twist: A Max Royster Mystery / Frank Hickey
1. Fiction - Crime 2. Fiction - Mystery 3. Fiction - Police Procedural 4. Fiction - Hardboiled

Published by Pigtown Books
ISBN: ISBN 9848810-0-0

For further information, please contact:

info@pigtownbooks.com

10 9 8 7 6 5 4 3 2 1

First Edition / First Issue

To Larry Hickey

1920 – 2011

# Prologue

Running shoes padded rhythmically along the soft dirt of Central Park's bridle path. A lone runner was pushing his slow way along the path, breathing hard and fast. Lamplight revealed a boy's plump sweat-streaked face beneath short blond hair. The leaves rolled over slowly, one after another, on the windy October night. The wind picked up again and then fell quiet.

The boy ran up a slight rise and leaped over a wide puddle, his face reflected in water the color of green tea. One more time he remembered how much he hated running. But his father made him do it.

Clods of dirt flew in his wake. He strained to go faster, each step pushing out the anger at his father. Then he let out his breath, winding down his speed from the sprint. His leg muscles quivered.

The wind picked up again. Turning, he walked back slowly the way he had come. Something moved in the grove of trees near him.

"Who –" he whispered out. "Who's there? Please!"

Suddenly afraid, he doubled his child's hands into fists. The silvery leaves stirred.

Someone sprang from the grove and slipped an arm under the boy's chin. The boy panicked as his legs were kicked out from underneath him.

"No! No! Please!" The boy's voice choked off. He felt himself spreading out on the leaves and dirt of the bridle path, smelling the warm bready smell of the attacker's body as he blacked out.

The strangler rode piggyback on the writhing, sweaty body and gave off sharp, piercing cries inside the crisp night air, like the yip of a small dog.

The strangler straddled the boy's body with long, strong thighs around his torso as the last breath of life choked out. Then the killer gave off a long, shuddering sigh and finally relaxed with a hand coming to rest lovingly against the dead boy's blond hair.

Weary after a kill, the strangler felt tempted to stretch out alongside the body and sleep, the only deep sleep possible now. But someone might find them.

Reluctantly, the killer rose and dragged the plump body farther away from the lamplight and under the trees.

# CHAPTER 1.

# NEW YORK CITY, 1995

Max Royster tooled the blue-and-white NYPD car through Brooklyn's back alleys, past broken toilets and gardens of scattered newspapers. He was a burly man with a shock of flame-colored hair. His thick buffalo hunter's mustache was the same color. He seemed much younger than forty-four when he smiled and his sparkling green eyes lit up his face.

"Try missing some bumps, Maxy," his partner, Hardesty, said. Hardesty boasted heavy forearms, with black fur that matched his eyebrows and five o'clock shadow. He was chewing gum and switching his cellphone on.

"Imagine waking up on this hellish street each morning," Max said. "It would sour a saint. No wonder everyone here lives loud and angry. The City of Pink People wrote off this black neighborhood before you ever hit the delivery room."

"Everyone says you talk funny for a cop, Max."

"Any unit, 2319 Lott Place, signal 10-17," the radio said. "Domestic violence. Female armed with knife, possible Emotionally Disturbed Person."

"Let's take it, partner," Max said. "Why not?"

"First, she might slice us with that knife. You already learned these politically correct bullets couldn't stop an EDP. Got cut before."

"Maybe she's calm now."

"Or we protect ourselves. That means the Duty Captain, Firearms Review Board, various angry reverends and newspaper columns. Jesse Jackson, Reverend Al calling us racists. Pickets in front of my house in Massapequa. My kids threatened at school. Maybe federal prison. All pointed at us. That's why not."

"You want someone else to take it?"

"Max, we haven't eaten yet. We're both starving. Collar her, we don't chow all night. 40,000 well-fed cops in New York, let them get energetic."

"We don't volunteer, they'll leave us alone?"

"Fine by me."

"You became a cop to get left alone?"

His partner cursed and speared the radio mike.

"Seven-One Eddie. Give us the job on Lott Place."

Still smiling, Max gunned the engine and whipped the car past two lumbering buses. Wooden frame houses splintered wearily into kindling on either side of the street. He slid to a stop near the address on Lott Place.

"2319's that crumbling apartment building on a rent strike," Max said. "No gas, water or juice this week. Squatters took it over."

Another NYPD car stopped. The driver, Yvers, a black woman, jangled out of the car. She waved her Glock 9mm gun.

"We'll take this job, Maxy," she said.

"Go assassinate someone else," Max muttered.

"Say again?"

"We got this job on paper, Yvers," Max said. "Cover the side. Okay? Thanks."

"Stop wearing a dress, Max," she said. "Use your piece for once. Just drop the stank bitch. Bang! Don't go fancy against a knife."

Max angled inside the dark lobby of 2319. Sweat sponged his dark blue uniform. Hardesty, followed, drawing his gun.

"Yvers already shot three citizens," Hardesty muttered, squinting into the corners. "Just got off Restricted Duty. Why does she always want to pull a trigger?"

"Goes back to her childhood. We don't handle this smoothly, she'll score Number Four."

"Only you care, Max."

"Stay clear for a shot," Max said, his voice shaky. "Give me room. I'll spray the bear grease."

"It better work. Can't see in here."

Max moved ten feet away, across the lobby. Afternoon sunlight poked through the wrapping paper taped across the broken windows. He gripped a Mace canister in his left hand.

Someone wailed from the staircase. Footsteps hammered. A huge black woman bolted downstairs. Blood smeared her shirt.

"See the devil!" she screamed. "See the devil everywhere!" She clutched a stained bread knife.

"Stay back!" Max shouted. He sprayed Mace at her. His other hand dug under his jacket.

The jacket snagged his thumb. He fought to clear his hand.

"Tear-gas!" she screamed, moving in. "Ain't nothing but aftershave!"

"Halt!" Hardesty shouted. He centered the 9mm two-handed on her belly. His trigger finger pulled back.

"The Devil, you!"

Max yanked the spray bottle from his jacket. He squirted it onto the floor in front of the woman.

Red liquid spurted out. The woman stepped onto it. Her foot flew out. She sprawled backwards. The knife slashed up.

"Max! Back up! Got a clear shot."

Max swung his baton. The baton smacked her knife hand. She screamed. She tried to stab him. The blade brushed his jacket.

"Max! Are you crazy?"

Max swung again and again. His neck veins stood out. The baton hit the blade.

The blade snapped and flew behind her. The woman scrambled up. She fell down again, gripping the broken knife handle. Her legs splayed out. Max's hands shook.

"Ma'am, you can't stand up," Max said. "Lie on your stomach, hands out in front."

She spat at him.

Hardesty moved closer and trained the gun on her.

"Max, don't try cuffing her. Get some backup."

"Like Yvers? Yvers'll blow her into rock 'n' roll heaven."

Max snaked out his handcuffs, waited and lunged. One handcuff snagged the right wrist. Max levered the steel against the bone.

"Devil, you're hurting me!"

"Give me the left, ma'am. Then it stops hurting. That way, everyone wins."

The woman got to a knee. Her foot flew out on the slippery floor. She sprawled again. Max crunched his teeth together, concentrated and caught the left wrist. He jammed it into the open cuff. Then he sank down, chest heaving.

She lay panting, handcuffed.

"Mace never works," Max said. "Karate would just make her mad. Tranquilizer gun will kill her. That slippery stuff knocks her down and keeps her down. God bless it."

"Where'd you find it, Maxy?"

"Thailand. Wild animal trainers use it."

"Someday, maybe our Department will okay us to use it."

# CHAPTER 2.

"I'm working for the city to make that money!" Max whooped as he left the precinct house. "I want that money! Whether you're rich or poor, it's always better to have money."

People did not laugh enough, Max claimed. Everyone took themselves too seriously. He was not important enough for that. Let them be serious somewhere else. He had worked and traveled around the world laughing.

He was starting to slow down now, though. Rich dinners showed in his thickening belly. It seemed like he had laughed more last year. Things had been better then.

"You're always talking this noise," Hardesty objected. They were coming down the precinct steps together. "Three times a day. After meals."

"That's because cash is important. Police work is not. Police work is something you Irishers dreamed up to chastise the non-Irishers you encounter in life and to sublimate you own huge sexual disappointments."

Max's precinct lay alongside Brooklyn's Prospect Park, the Flatbush neighborhood raped by crime and waiting to die.

Broad stone boulevards modeled after the avenues of Paris and narrow dead-end streets linked with wooden four-story bungalows tilted against each other. Here, thousands of poor black families were jammed on top of each other, paying high rents to live in the shells of old mansions as they crumbled and fell. Max looked over at the wide vacant lot across from the precinct house and whistled a scrap of a song. He whistled the same series of notes a dozen times a day. It was like a cigarette habit. The tune reminded Max of his ex-wife and it always made him a bit sad. Coming in or out of the precinct house, he would look at the blue and cream swirls of clouds, think of his wife and whistle that song.

"Try not to think about the Irish, Max," Hardesty said. "Can I buy you a Budweiser?"

"You may not." The two cops were heading for Topsy's Cocktail Lounge on Empire Boulevard, across from the 71st Precinct house. "But you may purchase me on or two fine cocktails. Maybe more."

They passed the spot where the Ebbets' Field baseball stadium had stood years before. In its place was an apartment complex, filled with families from Haiti, Jamaica or Mississippi, desperately trying to keep their families alive and off the streets before the Flatbush crack gangs claimed them.

As they entered the bar, other off-duty cops greeted Max and Hardesty with a nod or a wave of their beer-mugs that twinkled in the dim light. Max scanned the bar and took a deep breath.

"I care about money!" he announced. "Show me a man without money, and I'll show you a bum."

Tolerant smiles split the regulars' rough faces. They were all used to Max.

"What's that you call us?" Hardesty asked. "The tribe?"

"The Budweiser tribe. The orange-haired, pink-faced Irishers who always wear either bright Kelly green or hairy gray tweed. Or football jerseys. Who bellow and stomp around the local saloon like young prize whiteface bulls. Cops. Or priests. Con Edison workers, bus drivers or firemen. Irishers all. When you get older, you grow beautiful heads of silver and white hair. You can always see the tribesman on St. Paddy's day. Or at Topsy's here, sucking down those Budweisers so that the tribe carries on."

"Downright fascinating sociology," one of the other cops muttered.

"Devastating. Inspired." Chela, the statuesque black barmaid with her high swept crown of reddish hair, swayed closer. She wore a skin-tight leotard that showed her dancer's body. "Genius. But those big words must make you thirsty, Max."

"You're right. I'm dry. So I'll have a Beefeater martini with an olive and a twist. At least, I'm going to pretend that I have that money."

Topsy's was the local cops' watering hole. It was the only safe place to eat and drink in this ruined Brooklyn neighborhood, where crack gangs and hired killers ruled the streets. Rising crime and white flight had torn the heart and guts out of a neighborhood that had once been a sanctuary for working class families. Huge gaping tracts of empty land filled up with abandoned cars and dead bodies from the never-ending drug turf wars.

The martini was starting to push away Max's sadness. He caught himself looking out the window at the vacant lot and starting to whistle his song to himself, but he stopped in time. Hardesty was dickering for another round when a stranger in a dark business suit came through the front door and stopped in front of him.

"Excuse me," he tapped Max's shoulder. "Police Officer Royster, right?"

The man was about 30, with scrubbed Ivy League looks. He seemed very sure of himself. The other cops stirred, angered that a stranger was interrupting their Budweiser time.

"If you've got a subpoena for me, deliver it the way you're supposed to," Max answered. "To the desk sergeant at the precinct. But not here. That's not procedure. Play the game fair, counselor."

"No subpoena, Officer Royster." He waved a pink palm. "My client is suing you for false arrest, harassment, brutality and defamation of character." The lawyer seemed to be working himself up into a frenzy. "You like to misuse your pathetic little badge and authority."

He tossed his head angrily and his stylish brown hair slipped down over his ears. Max, sighing deeply, could smell hairspray.

"Leave me alone," he said. "This is not your courtroom. Please."

"I'm Martin Decker of the Brooklyn Legal Aid Society and I'm ordering you –"

"That does it!" Max howled, pointing a thick finger at the lawyer's hair. "That hair does it! Two rules of life, Martin. Never trust a man who combs his hair down over his ears. Or one who sprays it with stickum. Follow those two rules, Martin." He snapped his fingers.

"That's how you talk to a lawyer, an officer of the court? Well, I want to know something. Just what did they teach you at the Academy? Anything? Come on, tell me. What did they teach you?

Max let a sunny smile flower under his buffalo hunter's mustache. "They taught us, 'You don't fuck 'em after they're dead'," he said. "And that's all they taught us."

"THAT'S ALL THEY TAUGHT US!" the other cops chorused.

"It's going to be a pleasure putting you on the stand, Officer Royster," Decker said. "I can make you look real bad to the jury. Here's your subpoena. You're served."

Decker waved an envelope like a torch at the Olympics and smacked it down in front of Max's glass.

Decker turned, sneering at the row of cops.

"Hey, there, counselor," Hardesty objected. "Didn't you tell him 'No subpoena'?"

Decker turned to Hardesty.

"That's your interpretation, officer, not mine," he said and swept out of the bar.

"Don't sweat this noise, Max," Chela offered, taking the subpoena. "Not proper subpoena service." Expressive eyes glittered over her sculpted cheekbones. "Who is his client anyway? What's the deal here?"

"The deal is, his client is Desmond Reeves, who raped a girl on Lincoln Road last year. He's attacked three other women, served a year and was out on parole. Desmond was on crack this time. When we arrested him, he fought me, ran and fell, breaking his nose and arm. Old Desy claims back pain, too. He accused me of beating him with my stick.'

"Max, Max. You don't have a thing to worry about." Chela smiled.

"Oh, yes, I do." Max signed and spun the martini glass. "This victim withdrew her complaint because she didn't want her husband to know she had been raped. So the only thing we have on Desmond is resisting arrest. They can stick me behind a desk pending my Department trial."

Chela mixed him another martini while his buddies tried to help him forget. Underneath the sympathy was dread of the departmental reprimand and trial. The loss of pay, pension rights and a ruined reputation. Perhaps jail.

"I got to tell all you," Hardesty groped for the right word, "you boozebag lawmen, that Max has been my partner in this hellhole precinct for more than a year now. And I still don't know why he's working on this job."

"Neither do I," Max said.

"Did you really come into the job at forty-two?" a thin cop asked. His hair was done in crew-cut punk style and he had a diamond in his earlobe.

"Right," Max said. "The city lost my papers for twenty years so they had to let me on."

"And you were a chef in Hong Kong?" the cop shook his head. "Merchant seaman. Reporter in New Mexico. Wild Max, the gypsy."

"I do whatever the voices in my head tell me to do," Max said. "Different jobs, different countries, languages. But every-one's life has twists and turns. Some of us did heavy crimes before we turned cop. Nobody ever caught us."

"You're right on the money," one said.

"Some were aimed at the seminary from birth. They fell into this instead. Others were musicians. Some were born to be drunks. A few might have to go home every night and look at an orange while they jack off."

"They say you work too hard," Hardesty said. "But I'll ride with you anytime. Bear grease against a knife!"

"Citizens only pretend to be average," Max said. "To fit in. We're cops. We should know that."

In the back, the payphone rang. A sergeant scooped it up. "You, Maxy, telephone!" The sergeant, whisky-shaky after six hours of slamming them down, waved the phone at him.

"Justice League of America," Max sang into the phone.

The regulars kept woofing and grunting while Max listened.

"Chariot of justice rolling," Max said. He hung up the phone. "Goodbye, fellow sinners and publicans," he proclaimed to the beery fringe of sports jackets wobbling on whiskey legs.

"Yo, Maxy, are you okay to drive?"

"I'm not okay to do anything," he answered. "I just got ordered back into the street. This job is nothing for a grown man to take seriously."

# CHAPTER 3.

When he pulled up to the Central Park entrance at 102nd Street in Manhattan, Max saw that the entrance was blocked off by a pudgy Budweiser tribesman, with a corrugated pink face, wearing the NYPD autumn uniform.

Max fished out his nickeled police shield and flashed it.

"I'm on the job, officer. Sergeant Lipkin, Manhattan North Homicide told me to report forthwith."

"Okay," the tribesman said sourly. His face and his voice said he did not trust Max. Since Max was obviously off-duty and driving his own car, the tribesman figured he was on some special detail. He knew that an off-duty patrol cop did not usually show up on a detective sergeant's command.

"What's going on here? Why the roadblock?" Max asked.

"Ask your sergeant. He'll tell you." Angry at being stuck at this barricade all night with no dinner break, holding back information was his only joy. "Go ask him."

Max shook his head and drove his car up the sloping roadway, crossed the Park Drive North and went down a wide concrete strip. Two blue-and-white police vans blocked his way. He got out of his car and stepped off the concrete, immediately surrounded by thick oak and maple trees.

It was the wild part of Central Park. The land rose and fell sharply, showing unexpected hills and winding stone paths.

Everything grew freely here, unlike the fashionable and manicured areas downtown. It was more brooding, dark forest than city street.

"Get over here, Max," Sgt. Lipkin, a wrinkled leprechaun with a fine-boned face and thin sandy hair muttered. "I've got to protect you."

Creamy white lights clicked on now, catching the cops' cigarette smoke and making the place look like a movie set. At center stage, a naked, pale white body was jackknifed over some bushes. The star of the show. Max's mouth twisted downwards in a grimace.

The boy looked like some young sacrifice, offered while still fresh. The red meat of his thigh showed in the light, a raw glistening steak where the skin was ripped. Caked blood crusted the curved young thighs. The boy's sightless eyes were open and staring at the spotlight, at Max and the others grouped shamefully around the killing ground. Someone had enjoyed this disgusting act, Max thought furiously to himself, someone had killed this boy slowly and savored the act.

"Protect me from what, Al?"

Sgt. Lipkin's clothes hung loosely on him. He looked like he never got enough to eat. His speech was in the rough and sometimes high-pitched tones of Queens. Sometimes he sounded like one of the Bowery Boys.

"From all the bosses here," Lipkin replied. "They smell a big case, and they'll hurt you just out of nervousness. We've got some very nervous ones here tonight. Remember all those bullies in grammar school who used to put their knees on your chest in the playground? They all grew up and became bosses on this job."

Lipkin leaned against an oak tree as he continued.

"Of course, they're going to be nervous at the crime scene on a big one. They haven't done any work in the past two or three months. Just been coasting. And to cover that up, they might want to hurt an oddball like you. You're assigned to Brooklyn, not Manhattan. You're Patrol, not Detectives. What's that nickname you have for this neighborhood? What do you call it?"

"'The Playpen'," Max said. "The Upper East Side from 59th Street to 96th. I call it the Playpen because it is so well protected. Safe enough for children to play in. You could live and die in the neighborhood without ever having to see the real, the dirty side of life. If you stagger home dead drunk, a doorman will catch you before you fall flat on the sidewalk. Politicians, bartenders, businessmen and cops all cooperate to keep the Playpen safe for its wealthy inhabitants. There is no other neighborhood like it in the city. Maybe the world."

"That's why I whistled you up to help me," Lipkin said, grinning wolfishly. "Most cops cannot communicate with the residents of the Playpen. They are worlds apart. There is no common ground, Max. As a result, the investigation suffers. I can't let that happen to me, not on this case. You grew up in this neighborhood so you can talk their talk. You can liaison with them. You're the only cop in the city who grew up here. I checked. I need your help. That DNA stuff is still experimental. No way we could use it to ID this killer. Think over what you know about the place. Tell me anything you think I should know."

Max thought about the Playpen and the murders in this jeweled and affluent neighborhood. People here were killed because of the trouble that festered behind the tasteful brownstone walls and the well-dressed Playpen families. The murders always fascinated the rest of the city since the victims were so wealthy.

Max knew that there was a rich vein of trouble lying just below the chic surface here.

"He was about 15," Lipkin said. "Out jogging when he got killed. Judging from the leg muscles I felt, he doesn't run much. So he might have been using the run as an excuse to get out tonight. It's an expensive haircut. He looks like one of those private school kids whose families have a lot of jack."

"What would he be doing running up here?" Max wondered aloud.

"He's only a few blocks above the dividing line at 96th," Lipkin pointed out. "Below the line, it's safe. And he's got to run somewhere. So it looks like he ran the wrong way tonight and found the wrong guy. We're canvassing doormen on Fifth Avenue to see if they remember him. The way things are in New York, when a rich kid gets killed, it's automatically a big case. Someone rich and white got assisted from their troubles. 'Oh, mercy me. What's the city coming to?'"

"You think he's a private school kid with cash?"

"That's right," Lipkin answered. "Just like you used to be. That's why I called you."

He was silent for a moment, trying to decide how much to reveal.

"The killer chewed him," he finally added. "Some teeth lacerations around the groin."

Max winced.

"Don't ask me why," Lipkin said. "No matter how strange you feel yourself getting while you grow older, this killer is way, way ahead of us. Remember my lecture at the Academy? I'll repeat it for you now. 'Sexual happiness is the key to these killings'."

"You're saying that as a man gets older, he seeks newer thrills, newer jollies with this." Max touched his own groin through his blue jeans. "With his Mister Happy?"

"I'm saying that a sick guy needs the thrill, something new and exciting to keep him tickled,° Lipkin said.

"He needs some variety, the Gypsy Twist, whatever you're not getting at home from the steady hubby or little wifey."

The Medical Examiner's technicians were popping off soft white flashbulbs near the dead body. Close-up shots took in the pale pudding face and tousled blond hair. The harshly torn tissue on his groin gleamed where the teeth had ripped and torn. His lips showed blood. The victim had bitten his open mouth in terror.

"What kind of parent lets a kid run in the Park after dark?" Lipkin asked.

"The careless kind. The one who forgot what prowls this city after dark."

Max looked carefully at the dead boy, reminding himself that most murder victims looked very young and surprised when their bodies were found, as if life had suddenly rushed up and taken them unawares.

"When we find his family, Max, how do you think we should approach them?" Lipkin asked. "They're your people here."

"Whoa there, Al," Max's thick hands flailed around wildly. "You just said the wrong word. 'Think'? The Department tells me over and over again not to think. Just follow orders, they say. Keep the lid on and give out traffic tickets. The tail does not wag the dog. The Department will tell me when they want me to think."

# CHAPTER 4.

As Max and Lipkin watched, the detectives scribbled in their thin, bent cardboard notebooks. Their portable radios burped and growled, singing the songs on nighttime police work.

"All those empty suits," Max muttered, looking at the crowd of detectives. "I don't see any single one that's in good taste. Nobody knows how to dress in this Department. That's why they try to keep so many of us in uniform."

One of the bosses detached himself from the crowd and came over to Max and Lipkin, putting away his notepad and Bic pen. He was tall and heavy, with thick shoulders that seemed to push tightly against his dark blue raincoat. His hair was the beautiful silver-white hair that used to be the trademark of the old city cop, in the years when the Irish had dominated the Department.

"Lipkin? You on top of this here?" he snapped. "Got teams out canvassing, I hope. Grid pattern search, block-squaring method, all that shit you teach. We better find this mutt. Who's this?" he added, his tone implying that Max was another form of mutt.

"PO Royster, boss. He'll do liaison with me and the community."

The boss scanned Max up and down, taking in the bright green eyes and the smile lines. His patrolman's nose caught the scent of Beefeater martinis. This registered as Alcohol-On-Breath, a formal charge that he could level against any member of the service. That satisfied him. This jerk was an oddball cop that he could control by fear the same way he controlled all the others.

"Just so you know," he said, leaning into Max. "I'm Lieutenant Quinnliven, Manhattan North Detective Area, and I'll be in charge of this investigation. Sgt. Lipkin and all the others report to me. If you do anything, you fucking well better clear it with me first. No excuses. You'll do what I tell you to do. And I don't like people from other commands stepping all over my chart. No reason for you to be here that I can see. You got that?"

Max stared back. He could not help it. Quinnliven's pale blue eyes spoke of years of distrust. He was challenging Max, just like a street-corner drunk would challenge him during a late night tour.

"What'll it be, Royster?" Quinnliven asked. "You want to go back to whatever it was you were doing, or do you want to stay here?"

That decided it. There was no way that Max would let this tribesman talk to him that way.

"I'm staying, Lieutenant," he answered coolly. "There are things I can do on this case that nobody else can."

"Oh, yeah? You won't have room to goof off here. Nobody likes working under me."

Max paused, then said, "They just don't understand you the way that I do."

"Wise guy," Quinnliven replied mildly. "I'll speak with you about this later on, Lipkin. About your judgment in bringing this one in. But right now, we've got a possible notification. Family named Simmons called precinct to report their boy missing. East 94th Street. Go talk to the family. Don't let them contact the press. And don't breathe a word to anyone. We could be wrong. Or it could also be that one of his family killed him and is waiting for you to knock on the door so they can confess. Don't fuck up, you hear?"

Lipkin nodded and drew Max away from the lieutenant, closer to where they could both see the sprawled dead body again. The boy lay next to a large beech tree that had toppled over onto its side, roots eaten away by the loch waters. Its branches spread out thinly, like the scratchy fingernails of witches. Leaves crunched underfoot. More tree branches rustled in the wind, throwing light shadows over the dark path.

"Herb, if you please," Lipkin asked the photographer. "I'd like a couple of shots of that tree, with identifying data on the back of each shot." The photographer, a bald, mustached Crime Scene Unit detective, moved his enormous belly daintily out of his way as he reached down for a second Leica camera and nodded obediently.

"You're thinking that there may be a linking of images," Max said. "The boy is made to lie on his side the same way the tree lies on its side. The killer may have tried for a mirror effect and may not even be aware of it. Or it might be his personal mark, his signature, on these type of crimes."

"It's happened before," Lipkin said nonchalantly. He began walking towards his car. "I know that I asked you this before, but just how did you get through the Academy?"

"Sober merit. Sound family values. That's the thing about police work," Max drew out the words, "that-drives-me-wild. We do some of the hardest work in the city and some of the bravest but a boss with rank can make even the best of us tremble. It's like there's always a small, little-boy part of us waiting to be punished. You do it, and so do I. We avoid trouble with the boss."

They were in the car now and driving.

"Cool off, Max. You don't want to stay in Patrol forever."

"How true. I don't even want to stay a cop. I want to rob a bank."

"That's illegal. You can't do that."

"Why not? They rob me."

At 23 East 94th Street, they showed their police shields to the doorman. He was fat, with a quarrelsome, weak face, his bulk jammed inside a burgundy uniform. The doorman looked at the photo in Lipkin's hands and nodded.

"Yeah, that's the Simmons boy. Fourth floor. He went out dressed for running."

"How long ago?"

"Long time. I'd say three hours."

"What was he wearing?" Lipkin asked.

"Shorts, sneakers."

"Was he alone?" Lipkin pressed. "What about girls?"

"What do you mean?" the doorman asked.

"Come on. You know what I mean. Did he know about girls? Was he using the running as a cover to meet some honey?"

The doorman had given all he was going to give.

"He was just running, like I said. That's all."

"What about drugs?" Lipkin pressed. "Did you ever see the kid drunk? Or stoned?"

"Nothing like that. Never any drugs. This kid was straight. With my family, believe me, I would know."

A man and a woman, both elegantly graying and dressed in dark evening wear, drew near the building's canopy. The woman looked at Max's dirty blue jeans and then glanced away, reminding herself to be benevolent. The doorman stretched out his uniformed arm to open the front door for them.

His wristwatch showed just past nine. The questioning slowed down. The doorman remembered his job again.

Max sighed, suddenly feeling very weary, like he could hole up in a parked car and sleep all night. A lock of thinning red hair fell onto his high forehead. He felt the same kind of sadness as when he thought about his ex-wife. Suddenly, he felt like his insides had turned to mud, a thick, heavy mud that dragged him down and made each step hard to take. He hummed his scrap of melody, the same song that followed him everywhere.

"Are the Simmons home right now?"

"Follow me this way," the doorman said, walking towards the elevator bank. Max shook his head and followed him, still humming his song.

# CHAPTER 5.

Lipkin had never seen anything like the Simmons' apartment. The private elevator brought him and Max silently up to the fourth floor. There was no lobby. When the elevator came to a stop, Max pushed open the door and they found themselves inside the Simmons' front room.

The room was done in earth-tone masculine colors. Wide Oriental rugs covered the mahogany floors. The oil paintings on the wall looked like originals to Max's schooled eye. In the back of the room, a man half-rose out of a leather armchair. He gaped at Max and Lipkin as they stepped unannounced out of the private elevator.

The man's white hair lay carefully combed back, and he wore tortoiseshell eyeglasses halfway down his straight nose. From his demeanor, it was clear that this was an intrusion into his private world.

"We're police officers," Lipkin said quickly before the man in the armchair could say anything. "Are you Mr. Simmons, sir?"

"Who are you?"

"Police officers, sir. I'm Sergeant Lipkin and this is Police Officer Royster." Lipkin showed his gold sergeant's shield. "Who else is home now, sir?"

The man was moving more quickly than they expected. He had a weather-roughened, ruddy face, the kind that a sport sailor might have, and his hands were thickly developed.

"One of my daughters is asleep right now. I think the other one is reading. I'll have to ask you gentlemen to lower your voices. My boy is out somewhere. I'm Wendell Simmons. What brings you here?"

Max always hated to make death notifications. This one was even harder. Too close to home. The building, Simmons and the apartment all reminded him of growing up in this neighborhood. Max felt like he was coming home to tell his father the bad news. He did not want to tell Simmons about his son. So he stalled.

Lipkin was looking curiously at Max, expecting him to say something. But Max was frozen. It was clear that Simmons was within his own tidy world. Max knew that soon that would change forever.

Reluctantly, Max took the photo from Lipkin's hand and displayed it to Simmons.

"Is this your son, Mr. Simmons?" he asked.

Simmon's face slackened and lined as he saw the photo.

"That's Rusty," Simmons said. "Now, you go ahead and tell me what happened." The words came out of him sharply, with the voice rising. It was if he was scolding Max.

"Something happened, and he's dead, sir," Max looked into the mild eyes behind the tortoise shell glasses. "It was very quick. He felt no pain at all. He did not suffer."

"And just how did he die?" The voice was climbing higher now and starting to shake a bit. Simmons spun on his heel and grasped the top of the leather armchair. His red knuckles whitened.

"Was there anyone who wanted to hurt him?" Max asked gently, glancing at Lipkin. "Anyone at school? Anywhere else?" He eased himself over to a small antique chair and sat down gingerly in it. He wanted Simmons to feel more in control. Being in control might help him feel better. In order to do that, Simmons should be standing above him.

"He's only fifteen. No, sixteen now," the father's voice ground out painfully. "Sixteen in August."

"Mr. Simmons, why would someone want to hurt him?" Lipkin asked, finally able to talk. He had overcome his awe at the apartment.

"Was there any trouble anywhere? Jealousy? Maybe a girl or something?" Max heard slippery footsteps approaching from somewhere else in the apartment. He knew they would not have Simmons to themselves much longer.

"No, no," he drawled. Any shock that he felt was not showing on the surface.

Max knew that many businessmen who lived in the Playpen used the vague and forgetful manners of a grandfather to cover up what they really were. Max sized Simmons as a steely executive who knew how to push people around and break them if necessary.

"I'm going to call my lawyer," he said, "if that's all right with you."

"Whatever you want, sir." Lipkin put in.

"Let's go into my den," Simmons said. "We can talk more comfortably there, and we won't wake the girls."

They went down a mahogany hallway, and then they were inside Simmons' den. Max had been in this kind of apartment before as a boy, visiting his rich friends with their rarefied Playpen parents.

Simmons speed-dialed a number, apologized for the lateness of the call and asked his lawyer to come over. He did not explain why. Hanging up, he swiveled in his chair to face them again.

"Mr. Simmons, could we talk with you a bit about Rusty's friends?"

"I don't mean to be curt, gentlemen, but no. Not now. Think that it's best if we wait for my lawyer. Then we can talk."

Like hell, Max thought. Simmon's lawyer will tell him to clam up. These taxpayers told the Department what to do.

"Are you certain about that, sir?" he asked.

Simmons caught Max full in the face with own look. "Very sure, Officer Royster."

It was clear that if Simmons could remember names, he would be able to remember other things, too. They had to move very carefully with him.

"I hate to be a bother, sir," Lipkin said. "But could I use your bathroom for a minute? I'm sorry."

"Down the hall," Simmons pointed a thick hand. "Light comes on automatically as you shut the door."

Max knew that Lipkin would be checking the bathroom while he was in there. Looking in the medicine cabinet to see if Simmons used prescription drugs. He would learn who his doctor and pharmacy were. He would learn if anyone else had prescription bottles there. And he would sniff for any signs of drug use, with all the training of a shrewd cop who had spent a four-year tour in Narcotics.

"Is there anyone else you'd like to call now?" Max asked.

"Just leave me alone, Royster!" Simmons snapped, eyes lit and suddenly full of fury. "Don't con me with this!"

"What do you mean?"

"You know what I mean!" Simmons got to his feet. 'You know good and goddamned well what I mean. No, tell me this, instead. What did you do to him? What happened?"

"I didn't touch him. We don't know what happened."

"How did he die?"

"He was strangled."

"Not shot?"

"No, sir."

"He wasn't shot by one of you?"

"Sir, no cop was near him when he died."

"You burn them with stun guns," Simmons said. "Or you choke them with your nightsticks. Then the family is left to mourn. Don't tell me, Officer. I KNOW!"

"Sir, when he died, I was in Brooklyn. Mr. Martin Decker of the Brooklyn Bar was with me. Believe me, he will remember our conversation."

Simmons looked Max over, then he uncomfortably shifted his attention to an oil painting. "Excuse me, Officer," he said. "I feel like I've made a total ass of myself. "

"That's understandable."

"It was a dreadful accusation for me to make. Rusty's room is right here."

He pushed a door open and flicked on a light. It was a teenager's untidy bedroom, with thick athletic socks balled up on the blue carpet. Paperbacks tilted in rows next to the unmade bed. Two or three dirty white dress shirts were sticking out of a dresser drawer.

"If I can be of any help, Officer Royster."

"Max, please. My name is Max. Maxwell A. Royster. forty-four years old, divorced, of no noticeable morality, no cash and sleep in the raw."

Something inside the room caught Max's eye. A burgundy and white school pennant lay thumb tacked to a cork blotter on the wall. Saint Blaise's School. "Is that where Rusty went to school?"

"He was due to graduate in the spring."

"I went there," Max said. "Almost thirty years ago."

"You went to Saint Blaise's?" Simmons was surprised. "And you're a policeman?"

"It was a long time ago."

"And you became a policeman after Saint Blaise's. Was your father in the police department?"

"He worked in a print shop. They were giving out scholarships pretty freely back then. They hadn't discovered minorities yet. I scooped up a tuition deal and managed to get through. I didn't fit in there, but they let me hang around because I was amusing or something."

"They must have thought a great deal of you," Simmons said.

"They managed to keep their admiration under control. Most people do."

"This is very strange," Simmons said slowly. Then his eyes widened, as if he was realizing something. "You know, I can't believe he's dead." The words hung in the air. Max breathed out, watching him again and feeling awful. "I heard you telling me and I believe you but –"

Simmons put a thick hand up to his mouth, which was starting to tremble. Then his face crumpled as he cried, finally. He gripped Max by both arms as his own body shook and heaved back and forth. One by one, the tears moved down his face and fell on the rug.

# CHAPTER 6.

Lipkin was collecting the scraps for a murder investigation. Rusty's address book, snapshots for canvassing and a Saint Blaise's composition book that showed his childish handwriting.

Quinnliven and a fat black detective came up in the elevator. Quinnliven introduced himself briskly to Simmons, did not introduce the black detective and sent Max and Lipkin downstairs.

Max was glad to leave. He did not want to meet Rusty's sisters. They must have slept through Simmons shouting at him. He had seen enough for one night.

"It must have been a crazy," Lipkin muttered. "Some cuckoo bird out roaming through the park who just snapped loose when he saw the kid."

When they reached the lobby, several people had gathered around the doorman. The doorman swiveled his head around to signal that he needed them. Three men and a woman, obviously reporters, were trying to get around his uniformed arms. The papers would be sure to give this case the full treatment. He knew that he and Lipkin should avoid any publicity.

The reporters were trying to fast-talk their way past the doorman in the tense tones of go-getters working against a deadline.

"Hold it right there, ladies and gentlemen," Max said mildly. "Police officer. Nobody may enter unless they are invited. Just as you would want in your own home."

"Max! Max Royster!" This burst from the woman, a slim young redheaded reporter in a brown leather coat. "What are you doing here? Are you assigned to this case? Do you know the family?"

Lipkin made a warning noise deep in his throat. Max scanned the woman's fine-boned face with her large clear blue eyes, but he did not remember her. Her eyes looked as rare and delicate as prized family jewels, handed down from past generations. The rest of the press crowd paid close attention.

"Have we met?" he asked.

"At the Bastille Day party," she answered. "I'm Diana Calia from *The Daily News*. You were the chef at Roo Roo Turkewitz's party in July. And the you poured all the wine as the sommelier. No wonder you don't remember me."

"It wasn't a bad party," he said judiciously.

"Someone there told me you were a cop, but I didn't believe them."

"I have trouble believing it myself. Now, listen up, please. I know you've got your editors out there whipping you for a story. I used to be a reporter. But you're going to have to be patient. No statement is coming at this time. And no one, as I said, may enter this building unless invited by a tenant."

"That's what I tried to tell them," the doorman said.

"That's all right. We all understand that now," Max said in his deep, speaker's voice. It was the same way he calmed down family fights in Flatbush before anyone could get killed. "There's no more confusion now. Isn't that right?"

He looked meaningfully at the reporters.

They nodded like spanked schoolchildren. Like Max, they did not earn enough to live comfortably in the Playpen. They were allowed to work here only so long as they did not upset the working relationship between their publishers and the neighborhood powers.

"Officer Royster, Max, are you a friend of the family?" said Diana with the reddish hair. She was back to asking her reporter's questions again, the veins in her slender throat cording and standing out against the pale skin. Lipkin was getting nervous.

"There will be a press release coming out of the Public Information Section at One Police Plaza," he said. "You should contact them for that release. There won't be any statements or interviews here at this time."

Lipkin did not like the way the reporters were starting to fasten on Max. Looking him over. There were sure to ask the woman what she remembered about him from that party, at which he had probably been falling down drunk. And if they had nothing else on this story, they might try to make something out of that. They might ask Quinnliven why a rookie who was a heavy drinker had been assigned to a sensitive case like this one. Max was hurting him again.

"Where are you working, Max?" Diana took a step forward, coming closer to him. Max tried to cool himself down.

"71st Precinct in Brooklyn."

"That's a patrolman's badge, isn't is?"

"The term that we use now is 'Police Officer'," Max answered, looking Diana over amusedly. "The word 'patrolman' was deemed to be sexist some time back. We are now called 'Police Officer', which is unisex."

"You're not a detective, then?" the woman responded to his look. "If you're in a Brooklyn precinct, what are you doing here?"

"The same as always. I do what they tell me to do."

"Come on, come on." Lipkin said. "Contact Public Information. You all know the rules."

Max scrutinized Diana. She looked like a young jogger to him. She was probably half his age. He did not remember her from the party. He did remember cooking the cream and wine sauces that the French loved and singing Edith Piaf songs. It was always a mistake to get too wrapped up in your cooking.

"Look at her," Max said softly to Lipkin. "I've told you before how all we cops are really Irishers. Once we get through the Academy, we are Irishers. Even if our mommies think we are Chinese or Jewish. And Irishers hold their own devilish passions in check. Because we know about the huge, slumbering beer-soaked sheep dog of sensuality that lies sleeping inside the breast of every son of Eire. Look at her. That sheep dog must never be awakened. Because once it is awake and baying for its due, all things will fly to chaos."

"Easy. Slow down. Enough of this nonsense," Lipkin said. "You're talking trash. We have to get back to work."

Two uniforms came out of a blue-and-white patrol car. Lipkin stepped close to one and spoke quietly, too quietly for the reporters to hear.

"There's a Lt. Quinnliven upstairs, talking to the family. You know how you expect a lieutenant to be real prick? Well, he's that guy. He will be looking to hurt somebody tonight. Any excuse will do."

The uniformed cop, a wide, pale Irishman with raisiny brown eyes sunk deep in the pasty dough of his face, nodded. "You mean I'm in trouble just for being here? Maybe I'd better go on sick leave right now."

"Sure you could. But think of the next cop who gets assigned here," Max said. "The lieutenant would just nail him instead of you."

"That would be okay with me," the cop said. "I'm innocent."

"So is the next cop."

"Thanks for the word, guy. I guess."

Diana strode over to the doorman. "I'm with The Daily News," she said. "Whom did the police talk to in here?"

The doorman looked at her chiseled features and striking blue eyes. Then he shook his head.

"Come on, come on," Diana pushed. "Who owns this building? Didn't they tell you to cooperate with us? They could get some bad press otherwise. What's your name?"

The doorman looked over to Max, standing under the canopy. Max came over and looped his arm in a friendly move around the doorman's shoulders, knowing that now they were on the same side. The doorman patted Max on the back and wheezed. Max's green eyes lit up in mischief.

"You see how easily they can get you?" Max asked.

Lipkin steered Max away from the press and scandal. He was used to shielding Max from himself.

Max held Lipkin's radio. Fast talk crackled on it. Max's head jerked. Quinnliven stepped closer.

"Patrol got a hit," Max said. "Rooftop, 1185 Fifth Avenue. Let's roll."

"Who's giving orders here?" Quinnliven asked.

Max moved towards Lipkin's Cadillac. Lipkin hustled alongside.

"Street people crawl onto the rooftops here," Max said. "They dodge the doormen somehow. Sleep on the roof. Safe and quiet.

"Uniforms just found a violent rooftop cuckoo."

Lipkin gunned the engine. Max palmed the red police light and slapped it on the roof. The red light lit the well-kept streets.

They reached 1185. One blue-and-white angled next to a hydrant. The engine still ticked.

An old-time Irish doorman brought them up to the roof. His jowls shook and his soft pink hands trembled on the elevator controls.

"Come on!" someone shouted. "We don't want to hurt ya!"

Max stepped out from the penthouse lobby onto the gravel roof. The silver shield dangled from his belt.

Twenty feet away, a beefy homeless man spat and waved a hunting knife at two cops. He crouched on the edge of the roof. Caked blood and spit showed on his raincoat.

"Leave me!" he roared. "I'll cut you dead!"

One uniform, black, with a Fu Manchu moustache, trained his Glock on the knifeman.

"Back up a bit," Max said. "Whaddya got?"

"Checking the roof like the bosses want," the black cop said. "Found Nature Boy here."

"Gonna have to shoot him," the second cop said. Short, mustached and shifty, he squinted at the knifeman. "Tried talking him down for 15 minutes. Sale begins when the customer says, 'No'."

"Shoot him and we'll never know who aced the kid," Max said. "We need conversation, not assassination."

"Max, don't even think about talking him down," Lipkin said. He spoke into his radio.

"Manhattan North Homicide unit," Lipkin said. "Requesting Emergency Services, 1185 Five Avenue, rooftop. EDP with edged weapon, threatening MOS."

"10-4, Manhattan North," the radio said. "Be advised Emergency Services has a trapped child, lower Manhattan right now. Unknown ETA."

"Nature Boy ain't going to wait," Max said. He stepped along the gravel rooftop.

The knifeman roared. He slashed the knife in the air. Max's face tightened. He unsnapped the off-duty Glock. He held it behind his back. "What's your name?"

The man sunk back against the stone hut, roaring.

"My name's Max. What do you want?"

The man crept onto the narrow ledge. Below him, nighttime traffic slugged along Fifth Avenue.

He smiled. His mouth showed black rotting teeth.

"Come here," he crooned. "To me."

"Royster!" Lt. Quinnliven shouted, bulling onto the roof. "Fall back!"

"Can't now, Cap," Max said. "Scary enough just getting here."

"You'll have to gun him," Lipkin said. "Or he'll blitz you with that knife. Wait for ESU, Max."

"Get back here or you're in trouble!" Quinnliven shouted.

"Eighteen stories up, nut with a knife and me scared of heights," Max said. "Only some shots of pipsqueak 9mm rounds. What do you call trouble, Cap?"

Max unloaded his gun and jammed it in the holster. He slid the gun and holster 30 feet back to where Quinnliven stood.

"I'm quitting the Job now, Captain!" Max shouted. "Here comes the tin!"

He tossed the shield case underhanded to Quinnliven. It landed near the holster.

"Feels great to be a civilian!" Max sang out. "Now I can do real police work."

He moved along the rooftop. Gravel crunched.

The knifeman stood on the roof's edge. He raised one foot. Everyone watched him teeter. Max stepped within five feet. Lipkin aimed his own .38 at the knifeman.

"No good, boss," the black cop grunted. "This range, we'll just hit the cop."

"Ex-cop," Quinnliven said.

Max locked eyes with the knifeman.

"Tell me what you want," he said.

"Cut you good!"

"We already heard that song," Max said. "Sing another."

The knifeman edged along the parapet. A fire escape jutted up from below.

"Stay put," Max said. "No getting away now."

Max stepped up on the ledge. He blocked the knifeman from the fire escape. Slowly, he inched closer.

"Give it up, pal," Max whispered. "Nowhere to go."

The man lunged. Max twirled to his right. The blade nicked his left sleeve. Max wrapped both arms around the man's left knee. Max heaved. Both fell onto the gravel roof. The knife flailed.

The four cops pounded over the rooftop. The black cop kicked the knifeman's elbow. Something cracked.

"Ready to shoot, Mitchell!"

"No shooting!" Max hollered. He pulled the leg out, keeping the man down.

The cop swung again. The cop hit bone. The knife dropped.

The cops piled up on him.

"Get the left wrist, Sam!"

"Watch his teeth."

"Got the left."

"Slide it over."

"This joker's strong."

"Light-hearted, too."

"Freeze or you're dead!" Quinnliven shouted.

Quinnliven put his own chrome-plated big gun against the knifeman's ear.

"No contact with the piece!" Max shouted. "That's a rookie move!"

The knifeman grabbed the gun hand.

"My gun!" Quinnliven hooted.

The knifeman's fingers gripped the gun. Max struck the jaw with his palm. The man yelped. His hand dropped. Broken teeth tore Max's hand.

"O showers of bastards!" Max shouted. "That hurts."

Max's pinky finger showed blood.

"Mutt bit the cop's pinky."

"How come they never bite lieutenants?"

"Now the right," Max said. He slipped the handcuff over the sweaty dirt-stained wrist. The handcuff clicked.

The knifeman writhed on the roof.

"Maybe the good lieutenant don't know," the white cop said. "Never put your piece in close contact with a goony bird."

"That's enough!" Quinnliven barked. "You want a reprimand, officer bigmouth? Call for a bus. For the mutt. Royster's okay."

Tenderly, he holstered the big shiny .38.

"Two knives in one day," Max said. "Days fraught with imminent peril."

"Max, gets an AIDS cocktail from the ambulance," Lipkin said. "Every shot you can take. This fella don't look right with the Lord."

"First, give me back my gun and shield," Max said.

"No way!" Quinnliven said. "You resigned. We all heard it."

"Patrol Guide, boss," Max said. "'Any Member of the Service who does resign voluntarily, with no charges pending, shall have 24 hours in which to rescind his or her resignation. After that time period, the resignation shall become binding'."

"Forget it, Royster!"

"Rules, Captain. Would you like to explain to the Manhattan Duty Captain tonight why you broke the Guide rules? Gun and shield, Cap."

Quinnliven hawked and spat. Then he handed back Max's shield and gun.

"Now Al can interrogate this whiffleball at Bellevue," Max said. "And maybe I can slink back where I belong, doling out traffic tickets in Brooklyn."

# CHAPTER 7.

Max's long night was finally ending by the time he got back to his apartment on York Avenue. York showed traces of the Playpen's working-class past, with small neighborhood shops and taverns jammed in beneath new high-rise towers. It was morning, with the sky a dirty gray over the East River. Nobody was up and moving at this hour, except night workers, wandering crazies and the metal-groaning garbage trucks wheezing and slamming over the sidewalks.

As Max climbed up the stoop, he stumbled once from exhaustion. His body aches had grown worse as the night had dragged on. He remembered that his tiny apartment looked like a train wreck, and he did not want to face it right now.

Max wanted to forget what the dead kid had looked like. Remembering how Rusty's father had looked as he finally absorbed the news had been bad enough, the seamed and gentle face tearing itself apart.

He looked over his shoulder at the East River, two-hundred yards away, the churning waters of what the tug-boat men call "Hell Gate." The tides here were the worst in the city. According to New York lore, any swimmer who tried to stay afloat there would drown in minutes.

Max wanted to walk by himself along the riverside until he was tired out and then fall into bed. Or maybe he would just fall into the water. That would bother nobody very much at all, he figured. He started walking.

"Hey, Max! Hey, you! Wait up for me!" A young woman was moving quickly across the sidewalk toward him, her hair flying in the river wind. Max turned clumsily, startled, and recognized the reporter who had grilled him outside the Simmons' home. She looked even younger and slighter than she had before. She was wearing a dark blue jogging jersey, jeans and running shoes.

"Good morning! Good-bye! I'm not talking to the press."

"Don't be such a prig," she said breathlessly, catching up to him. "You're such a prig. How do you know that I don't just want to talk to you? Just to you."

Her fine blue eyes caught his and would not let them go.

"I'll take that chance. How did you find me? That interests me more," he said.

"Easy. Roo Roo Turkewitz still treasures your phone number and address."

"How is dear old Roo Roo? So she fed me to you."

"That's not the way I would put it."

Max fought against the light-hearted stirring inside him and scrutinized Diana again.

Her eyes slanted down slightly against high cheekbones. Her face was as pretty as a cameo, with smooth model's bones molding through the fair skin. Her hair was not bright but a very dark reddish color. It hung heavy and glossy over her exquisite face.

"How come you work for a newspaper?" he asked bluntly, moving his hand with the bandaged pinky finger.

"With your beauty, you'd make three times a newspaper doggie's salary on TV."

"I'm not a TV talking head," she returned. "My family is Sicilian and Finnish and they stuck me with a work ethic that I cannot shake. When a story interests me, I will do anything to write it."

"You're pretty young for 'anything'."

"And you're starting to interest me again. Forgetting about the story. I'd listen to you for free."

"You're cuckoo. Whether you're rich or poor, it's good to have money."

Max studied the water smashing over the rough stone jetty. "Wonder if I belong in cop work," he said. "Little by little, I could snap my cap. My dreams sing the blues now. Despair could be the only answer."

"Living alone doesn't help," she said. "You know, someone butchered a rich schoolboy in New Orleans last year. It was very similar. The victim was cut and strangled. My computer search turned it up. When will your Department send someone down to tie that killing to this one?"

"When cats bark."

"So they don't care about finding this killer. What do they care about?"

"Lunch. The NYPD figures that whenever you send a cop out of town, he guzzles rivers of whiskey and paws every woman possible. On city pay. No boss will risk signing that order."

She nodded. He blinked back the tears again, hummed his ex-wife's song and shook his head. His eyes were turning bloodshot from the long night.

"You know, we are not so very different from each other," she said. "Cops and reporters in this city have a lot in common. We both know the city's secrets. We write about them. You solve them. A lot of reporters desire the emotional and physical courage to become detectives. Some policemen wish they had the education to become reporters."

"Good hook," Max smiled. "To get me interested and talking back to you. It may even be true. But no cop's winging to New Orleans on your idea. Because your interest in this killing is transitory. Temporary. What's tomorrow's story?"

"What'll you do tomorrow?"

"Right," Max said. "Patrol. Family fights and crack overdoses. I'll be doing what I always do."

"What's that, Max?"

"I do what they tell me to do. I sign log books. I listen to my supervisors. Follow the chain of command. Grub for overtime."

He broke off and shook his head. She was making him talk too much.

"I'm cold. I shouldn't be talking to you this way.

A tugboat named the Elizabeth-Janeth was pushing its way against the Hell Gate current. The deckhand, wearing a scuffed brown leather jacket, sat contentedly near the stern.

"Everyone whom I know with a column achieved that column because they were angry," she said. "So they steamrollered everything that ever got in their way. I've been churning through stupid scut-work stories since I graduated. And I'm furious enough to get my column now."

"You look it," Max said. "Something in your face. Women are much harsher than men. Tougher fighters, too. My ex-wife taught me that. She could have assasinated me during the honeymoon."

"I am glad that your marriage taught you something important."

"I'm cold," Max repeated. "Enough of this exhilarating promenade. I'm going home."

But he did not move.

"C'mon. I'll buy you a cup of coffee."

"I don't need it," he said. "And I've got a hand grinder in my apartment for coffee."

"I accept," Diana said simply. "Let's go there."

"It wasn't an offer." His body opened up, like a long shout across a windy valley, to tell him how tired he was now. He was too tired to think straight and he wanted to get away and toss himself to sleep in his apartment. "I'll see you around."

He hustled away from the river wind, turning his back on the slim figure in blue jeans by the sea wall.

"Hey, Max! You remember my name?" she called after him. "Diana! Okay? I'll be in touch with you. Roo Roo told me all about you!"

# CHAPTER 8.

Saint Blaise's School for young men occupied three connected brownstones in the East Eighties, off East End Avenue. The block was usually a quiet and sedated one. But twice a day, at eight-thirty and three-thirty on weekdays, it exploded when boys wearing blue blazers with the white and burgundy Saint Blaise's goldthread patch on the breast pocket came bursting out of the school's doors.

"Make you feel funny, going back in?" Al Lipkin asked Max as he parked the squad car.

"You know I hated the place."

"You keep mentioning that to me in saloons. But I need you nice and cool on this one now."

"I'll be cool. Just don't let them put me back in Mr. Thompson's Latin class."

They went inside the front entrance. Outside the headmaster's office, a tall, thin receptionist with mink-colored hair piled high on her head and an English accent asked if she could help them. Lipkin gave his name and asked if he could speak with the headmaster. He was being careful about his speech.

Max looked at the quiet elegance of the school. It appeared as if nothing had changed since his graduation.

Then the office door opened and he felt a small shock, like he was stepping back in time.

"Mr. Lipkin?" The man coming through the doorway loomed bulky and large, with thinning gray hair gathered carefully over his scalp. His voice was the voice of a public speaker, deep and sure of itself. Bright blue eyes scanned Max and Lipkin from behind expensive eyeglasses. He wore a well-cut black pinstriped suit, making him look like a high-priced trial lawyer. The skin over one cheek was tightened and scarred. Max remembered a story about acid spattering onto him during a science experiment.

"I'm Trumbull Pruitt, the headmaster," the man said, motioning them inside. "Please make yourselves comfortable."

The two cops both seated themselves in his office. Lipkin wore one of his anonymous gray suits with a light blue dress shirt and a narrow red necktie. Max wore a dark tweed jacket that he had bought in the Cancer Society Thrift Shop for four dollars, his usual blue jeans, a torn white dress shirt and tan suede desert boots.

"We need to speak with you about one of your students," Lipkin began.

"Rusty Simmons? The boy who died last night?"

"Yeah, that's the one. How did you hear, if you don't mind my asking? I didn't think that the news had been made public yet."

"One of the parents called me this morning. Before your officers did. He died in the park while he was running, they said."

"Yes. He and his father lived near the Park." Lipkin looked abashed. He was out of his element and he knew it.

But Pruitt was at home in his office. As a private school headmaster, he looked out over the territory of books and minds and juvenile behavior.

"Can you remember who telephoned you with the news?" Lipkin asked.

"I don't see why that's important. Who called me, I mean." Pruitt turned to Max, who had not yet said a word. "By this afternoon, it will all be public information."

Max had never been able to relax in this office. He saw with some pleasure that Lipkin, so relaxed in the police world, would never be comfortable here, either, but for different reasons.

"You wouldn't remember me, Mr. Pruitt," Max said. "But I was one of your students here. I even graduated. Since then I blundered everywhere and finally turned cop."

"A Saint Blaise's boy is a policeman?"

"Everyone asks that same question. You were the assistant headmaster back then and taught us religion. My name's Max Royster."

Pruitt scrutinized him, flipping through the thousands of shining young faces stored away in his memory. He shook his head.

"It's been such a long time, Officer."

"I came in on a Drake Scholarship," Max said. "One of the first ones. And I was a discipline problem."

"'Was?'" Lipkin asked.

"Of course," Pruitt settled back in his chair, "I remember you now. Max Royster. You were suspended twice, weren't you? You've changed so much. You dropped out of City College, I recall. This is a surprise, you as a policeman. Somebody told me you were working as a chef in Hong Kong. Then you taught school."

Lipkin had wanted Pruitt relaxed. He saw with satisfaction that his plan was working.

"Mr. Pruitt, who were Rusty's closest friends?" Lipkin asked.

"Al, I have an idea," Max said, irritating Lipkin. "If it suits Mr. Pruitt, perhaps instead of asking questions piecemeal, we could speak with each other in private. That's the best and most sensible way for us to work. Mr. Pruitt, can we have the teachers come and talk to us?"

"Of course. Use my office, please." Pruitt smiled wryly. He went to the door and then turned. "By the way, Mr. Lipkin, you didn't tell me how Max is doing as a policeman. Is he avoiding trouble, I hope?"

Lipkin shrugged, searching for a tactful response. "No one will ever forget Max," he said.

"Maybe I shouldn't ask, but I'm curious."

"The Department is still trying to figure Max out," Lipkin allowed. "But we're a large outfit and we've always had our share of unusual types and visionaries."

"Madmen and dreamers," Max chirped. "That's me."

# CHAPTER 9.

They began by interviewing teachers. Lipkin took the lead and spoke like he always did, asking questions in a casual, offhand manner. His years of technique were well hidden beneath the surface.

The first teacher was a history expert, a quarrelsome frog of a man in his sixties with a brisk manner and a sharp tongue. He seemed to have his mind elsewhere while they talked. The next person was a tall, willowy blonde woman in her early twenties with dark eyes. Neither of them had known Rusty well.

As the day wore on, the chain of teachers continued. Some knew him as a soccer player on the school's third-string team. Others noted that he had been a poor math student. His chemistry had been nonexistent.

One teacher, Mr. Mulhearn, remembered Max's face as soon as he sat in the armchair. Mr. Mulhearn had altered very little in twenty-six years. St. Blaise's was not the kind of place where things changed.

Max remembered that the teacher's salaries had been very low. He and his pals in the seventh grade used to follow their teachers home to see where they lived. Max learned how hard it was to follow somebody on city streets. The teachers' apartment buildings had looked plain and drab. But the teachers had liked the Playpen's style, and they liked to live near the rich. Sometimes they copied the rich.

"I'll be glad to speak with you about Rusty," the next teacher said. Her hair was cut stylishly short and she wore thick eyeglasses. Suddenly, tears were rolling down from her quiet brown eyes. Max looked closely at her and saw that she was weeping freely without any tremor in her voice. It was as if she were trying to staying calm.

"I'm sorry," she said, ducking her head low to hide the tears. "It's just so awful. And I miss him already. This whole thing happened so quickly. It seems like all I can do is cry."

Max did not know what to say. Lipkin was hanging back. Reminding himself that this was Max's job, to handle the rarefied Playpen types.

"When you work as a teacher, you don't think that something like this will happen," she said. "You worry about protecting the boys while they're in the classroom. You never imagine something like this."

"It may be a random killing. Or it may be someone who knew him," Max said. "We have to find out as much as we can about Rusty. That's the important thing now."

Talking to this teacher bothered him somehow. She was different from all the others who had covered up whatever emotions they felt. This woman was the first one to cry and it made Max feel sad to watch her.

"I'm going to talk with my boss here for a minute," Max told her. "Check our office for messages and all that stuff. You just relax here and we'll talk again if you want to."

"I can talk now," she said. "It doesn't matter how bad I feel."

"It does to me," Max said. "Take five. There's plenty of time."

Lipkin made a face and they went out into the hallway together. Lipkin looked around guiltily before lighting up a Camel.

He was sure that smoking was forbidden here.

"Since when am I your 'boss'?" Lipkin asked, cupping the Camel. "Whatever you did to her, it sure turned on the faucet."

"She's just crying. There's a lot to cry about."

"You're telling me."

"Something about her makes me nervous," Max said. "Like she might fly apart. Why don't you talk to her?"

"That's why I've got you here. You're the hometown favorite around this school."

They went back inside Pruitt's office. The teacher was still in her chair. She smiled faintly at Max, and he felt the hysteria just beneath her surface. But she had stopped crying now and seemed much calmer. Now he could see how pretty she was, especially when her face relaxed into a smile. If he had seen her at a party, he would have paid attention to her and tried to draw her out.

"My name's Max," he said. "What's yours?"

"Lily Sangster. I was Rusty's homeroom teacher. I also taught him English and History."

"Ms. Sangster, our only reason for disturbing you now is to find out about Rusty. You were his teacher, and you helped him. That's what we're trying to do now. Help him. We're all working together, aren't we?"

She nodded and her black hair dipped. She moved a hand across her high cheekbones. Max hoped she would keep calm.

"Is there any reason that you can think of that this might have happened to Rusty?"

She shook her head. The eyeglass lenses reflected the lights in Pruitt's office.

"If you taught him English, you probably have compositions he wrote. We would like to see them. Is that all right with you?"

"Of course it is." Her voice was so soft that Max could hardly hear her. She was tall, just a few inches less than Max's six feet. The dress she wore was loose fitting and gray, of a fine silk material that effectively masked her body. She slouched as if she were trying to hide her height. Max guessed that she would find it difficult to handle a classroom of hooting young boys.

He thought again how if they had met somewhere else, he might go to her apartment for a nightcap. She intrigued him. There were no rings on her fingers. She had square, competent hands. Her eyeglasses were expensive, the type called "fashion eyewear" in the Madison Avenue boutiques nearby. From the thickness of the lenses, Max thought she must have to wear them all the time.

"The radio said it was a mugger who killed Rusty. Is that possible?" Lily Sangster's voice was educated. Unlike some of the other teachers, her voice had no trace of a New York accent.

"Like I told you, Ms. Sangster, anything is possible." Max smiled at her, hoping to keep her calm. "Just the way you tell your boys what to do, the Department tells me what to do. They give me no reasons. They told me to come here."

Lipkin did not like Max talking this way to a civilian and cut in impatiently.

"Is there anything more you'd like to tell us about Rusty?" he asked.

When she turned to face Lipkin, her face dimmed. Talking to Max had livened her up for a moment.

"No, sir," she said.

"Thank you very much for your time, then," Lipkin said. "I just have one question," she said, rising gracefully from the chair. "Mr. Pruitt said one of you went to school here."

"Guilty." Max raised a hand. "I'm that guy."

"Ah, yes." Lily scrutinized him. "Yes, I can see that," she said.

ஐ

The next few teachers took less of their time. Gradually, a portrait of Rusty emerged. He had been a shy, frightened boy just beginning to move through the teenage world. But there was nothing to interest either cop. When they had talked to all his teachers, Pruitt welcomed them back to his office.

"This might be one of those serial killers, right, gentlemen?" Pruitt asked. "Someone who kills for no apparent reason. Don't they travel a lot to find victims?"

"Not always, no." Lipkin answered. "Ed Gein never strayed far from the Plainfield, Wisconsin, hotel where he found his victims. He was the one that Hitchcock made the movie *Psycho* about. John Gacy did not travel. A lot of times, the victims come to the killer."

"And there's not way to discover these monsters?"

"I'm no expert on serial killers. I don't even think the Department has one. These killers indulge their fantasies and when they're through, somebody's dead. That's all I know."

"Most murders happen to street people," Max added. "And they show us that the killers know their victims. But with a boy like Rusty, these methods of finding the killer are useless. That's why we're here."

"Do you think that he was killed by a stranger?"

"We don't know," Lipkin said. "It's easy to strangle someone. I hope people never learn how easy it is. Serial killers are not your regular murdering slobs in a beer joint. Their kills looked random to the outside observer. But to the specialist, each victim fit a particular pattern. They all had something in common."

"I hope it wasn't Saint Blaise's that triggered this killer," Pruitt said. His fingers drummed a thick book.

Neither Lipkin nor Max said anything. They both knew that it was a possibility, and that if they were dealing with a serial killer, more boys like Rusty might be in danger.

"The FBI estimates that there are five hundred serial killers on the loose," Lipkin said. "Catching one is rare. We know so little about them."

"It's disgusting," Pruitt said and turned to Max. "Are you going to be a policeman for long?"

"Not if I can get into banking."

Pruitt shuddered. It was as if by changing the subject, he could shake off the feeling of gloom.

"Max is being modest, Mr. Pruitt," Lipkin said. "He did not just wander everywhere. He's a self-educated man of the world who was a Hong Kong chef, New Mexico reporter and boxing coach in Mexico. Where was your boxing gym again, Max?"

"Guanajuanto, Mexico. It was fun getting kids into shape. I was doing something positive. Which is more than I can say about police work."

The headmaster got up and moved around his office. In one corner, there was a polished wooden valet dresser standing six feet high. It was designed to hang clothes up in their creases and keep them crisp. Pruitt's raincoat hung from it. He tapped the polished wood with his palm.

"Sergeant, I'd like the precinct to assign a policeman to walk a beat around the school. Will you help me with that request?"

"If you think it's necessary," Lipkin answered cautiously. He knew Quinnliven would be angry about the request. The lieutenant did not want this neighborhood frightened by the killing. "But I think this is just a random killing. It probably has nothing to do with your school."

## CHAPTER 10.

At three-thirty that afternoon, the boys from Saint Blaise's flowed down the school stairways and out into the street. Someone had a football, so two teams grouped up for some two-handed touch on the concrete. Other boys moved toward Central Park, hooting and skylarking.

The air smelled like rain. The sky was pure oyster white. A chill wind was pushing across the flat meadow where people played softball and soccer next to the gray stone Belvedere Castle. The waters of Turtle Pond lapped nervously. A small tan and white mutt skittered in and out along the muddy shore, playing along the edge.

One of the Saint Blaise's boys crossed over the playing fields, shouldering his leather book bag. He was dressed in a school blazer. White-soled Topsider moccasins showed under gray flannel slacks.

"Blake! Where are you going?" his friends called, bouncing a soccer ball. "We're choosing sides!"

"Choose up! Choose up!" the schoolboys shouted, their tony accents carrying across the fields. "Let's get teams!"

"I'm the goalie!" one of them chirped, tossing down his blue blazer.

"Who's the ref?"

Blake wandered off the field by himself, into the fringe of bushes. When he heard his name called, he turned.

The boys booted the ball downfield for the first move. The fullback trapped it and kicked it back to their front line.

Suddenly, a car's harsh engine buzz-sawed. The boys saw a battered tan car lurch out of the shrubbery, dragging something behind it.

The car tore across the playing field. Blake screamed. A chain lashed tight around his chest held him to the car's back bumper. He shrieked as he slammed into the ground.

The schoolboys wailed helplessly as they glimpsed the meat of his chest wall tearing easily open, spilling rib bones out carelessly onto the soccer field.

Then the chain loosened and the boy's body spun to a stop, a smoking, dripping haunch of red beef, slowly tipping to fall onto one side.

## CHAPTER 11.

Lipkin arrived at Max's apartment and roused him with the bad news. They were both on the park playing field within twenty minutes. Some of the same cops who had been on duty last night were still there, tired and unshaven. Lipkin looked briefly at the dead boy's body, the expensive rags of clothing stained with blood. He walked to Lt. Quinnliven and stood by him respectfully.

"We have something very odd here," Lipkin said. "The teeth marks from last night's victim were those of a woman. Today, two joggers saw a white woman driving this car that killed this boy. It looks like we've got a female serial killer. And I have another lead, pointing to a woman. Someone, one of my snitches, called me about an *au pair* girl who took care of wealthy kids. Her name was Charlene. Her references sparkled. The mommies smiled at the way she took care of children."

Lipkin sighed. This case grooved his face with pain lines.

"One night, the daddy came home early to find Charlene using his ten-year-old kid for sex in the bathtub. Doing things that I never heard of. Weird stuff. Daddy-o freaked out. Charlene fractured daddy's skull against the bathtub and fled for parts unknown."

"Any complaint on it?" Quinnliven barked.

"Cop question," Max muttered.

"From those movers and shakers?" Lipkin asked. "Dream on. They never stand in front of a precinct desk and wait for someone to help them. They'd call a squash buddy who knows the Commissioner."

"So then what happened?"

"The family felt too ashamed to step forward. Publicity could destroy the kid. Make it tougher for him to court some rich little Muffy for the wifey slot. No, they buried it with the discreet greenbacks."

"Can you reach this snitch who called you?"

"No chance. I don't know jack about her. My mystery lady. Only calls from payphones. This family hushed it all up to protect their son. The father took a position with his company overseas. I'm trying to trace them now."

"What's that word *au pair* mean?" Quinnliven asked.

"Babysitter. And Max said someone aced a New Orleans rich kid. Similar killing. We should fly there to check it."

"I never heard of a female serial killer," Quinnliven said. "And nobody's flying nowhere. You better be sure, Lipkin. Why do you think this Charlene broad is our killer?"

"Her attitude. She wanted to work around the rich."

"So do a lot of people. Does anything physical match?"

"Not yet."

"Then keep your theory to yourself. And New Orleans. That's an order, sergeant. I'm not hitting the panic button that someone's on a rampage against private school boys without more evidence. You've got to be kidding. If the public ever heard that!"

Quinnliven started to walk away with a closed face.

"Lieutenant," said Lipkin. "If I could get one of our sketch artists to speak to the people that Charlene worked with. Just as a routine thing. We could use a sketch of her for now, if only for the purpose of elimination."

Quinnliven shook his silver-white head and strode away. Years of paramilitary service struggled in Lipkin and finally won out. He stayed quiet.

"Well, it's nice to know the lieutenant's on our side," Max said briskly, stretching his mouth in a wide, meaningless smile.

"Come on, Max. I don't need that. You and I used to be close. What's happened to you?"

Max shrugged. He tugged his own red hair cowlick. "Sorry, Al. You're right. If you think that Charlene is our killer that's good enough for me." He glanced over at the body. "Look at that poor kid. He looks like a fire sale on orange marmalade."

Lipkin shook his head, looking after Quinnliven's retreating raincoat. "Something must be bothering him. This isn't like him. Must be something wrong."

"Sure. He's a swell guy. And if he's having a bad day and takes it out on you. Just shrug it off. I wish I could. It doesn't matter that our case suffers, and the killer may kill another kid because the lieutenant is feeling childish and bitchy today. His feelings are what count. Because he's got the rank."

"Be serious, Max."

"Al, I tried being serious. All I could get was construction work."

"Stop talking trash." He shook his head again, then slipped back into the workaholic style. "Let's get some teams out canvassing."

"Wait a minute, Al. Let's think about this first. You can't match up anything with Charlene because you don't have anything physical about her, do you? No fingerprints. No hair samples. There is no way you can tie her to these killings."

"Like I said, it was just her attitude. She wanted to work near the big bucks. The au pair agency she worked for remembered that clearly. She only wanted rich families to work for. She became angry when they could not place her with the wealthy. That stuck the agency head as bizarre."

"Sure. The rich titillated her. They do that to a lot of people."

"Later, after Charlene attacked the father, she showed up at the agency to get her application. They dialed 911 and she ran. That night, someone broke into the office and tried to get her file. But they could not get inside the locked cabinet. It was Charlene all right, trying to cover her trail."

"How about us getting her file?"

"The agency is afraid of a lawsuit from the kid's parents. Their lawyer told them to dummy up and produce no records without a subpoena. And we can't get a subpoena without Quinnliven."

Max grimaced. "How does a man like that get to be a Lieutenant of detectives running a homicide case? How does he even get to be a police officer? Look at him. He's got a head on him like a butcher's dog."

"Max, he's your superior officer."

"Woof, woof!" Max said. "Bow-wow, Lieutenant Doggy. Okay, so we can't go that route. But before we start canvassing, let's call upon the Parks Department. Get a list of all the employees who worked near here today. Call them at home to see if anyone noticed a car parked here. Somebody must have. You need a Parks Department plaque showing before you can drive off the roadway here."

He saw Lipkin's hesitation.

"Do it, Al," Max said. "The killer used a car. That's the only thing that we're sure of now. All the other facts will have to come from that one."

"Charlene was a false name," Lipkin mused, snapping out a Kent cigarette from his breast pocket. "After the attack, the agency checked her references. All phony. Everything about her was false. After she split, she went way, way underground. She just vanished. She's faceless now, a young white woman, and there is nobody who can identify her."

"The other parents at the *au pair* agency would remember her. Wouldn't they talk to you?"

"How do I find them without the agency's help? These people are exclusive, Max. Private. Soft-spoken and well heeled. There was never a criminal complaint filed against Charlene. On paper, she never existed. Memories fade. She could move around this city for the rest of her life and not worry about getting caught."

Max looked at the darkening greenery again and tried to imagine Charlene moving silently through it all, planning her next kill. Was she one of those love maps had gone wrong, whose warm childhood feelings of sex had gotten twisted up somehow with pain? Out on the street, underground as Lipkin called it, she would never be able to untangle it. Max hummed his piece of a song again and remembered how his ex-wife's eyes and hair had looked when she was in one of her rages.

"I was right in what I told Diana the reporter," Max said. "Women can kill more easily than we men. This kill proves it."

"They want you back at your precinct at eight tomorrow morning," he heard Lipkin saying. "There's nothing I can do about it. They keep ignoring me. But I'll get you back here."

"Without any sleep? I'll be dragging ass all day tomorrow, as it is. Hardesty will have to drive. And who says I want to work here? Things are easier in Patrol. Why don't you just give me a good leaving alone?"

"Do you want more little schoolboys to die?"

# CHAPTER 12.

They both fell silent. They had reached the dead end road that used to be their friendship. Lipkin respected and loved the Department as his only true creed. He would obey the policies as the only way to stop slaughter. Max laughed at the same Department and suffered through all the pettiness.

Max kept staring at the gradually darkening Park, finer and subtler than any artist's hand could have sketched. Shadowed shrubs, with somber lines deepening as the day's light faded. These were the footpaths where he and his friends from Saint Blaise's had once roamed. When they were nine-years old, they roved in packs, each of them trying to make the most noise. After they turned twelve, they had often felt the need to walk the same paths alone at night, singing to themselves when they were sure that nobody could hear:

> In delay, there lies no plenty,
> Then come and kiss me, sweet and twenty!
> Youth's a stuff that shan't endure!

Rusty Simmons must have felt the same need, to walk alone.

Maybe he had been doing that when he died. What could have driven him to be alone in the park last night? Perhaps his family might know.

"The patrol guys were left at the murder scene," said Lipkin, breaking into Max's reverie. "They said somebody was nosing around the scene, where it was roped off. The city is starting to get curious, Max. Soon as this story hits, they'll panic. I want to head up to the crime scene now."

As they drove north in Lipkin's Cadillac, they looked carefully at the people bicycling or jogging along the park roadway. Max tried to look again at his greenery but it was too dark now to see much. It was the start of evening, the soft hush of the sun being wrestled down and strangled slowly by indigo. And a hush rolled out of this sunset. The hush gathered strength in the darker precincts of the park, where things were more primitive and closer to the earth.

"You told me that roughly a third of the people now living in the Playpen were raised here," Lipkin said. "That the Playpen is slowly dying out as a rich neighborhood because the other two-thirds move away."

"It's true," Max agreed. "In ten years, the Playpen may not exist anymore."

"But even with the high rents, some middle-class people live here. I know nurses and cops that live here. They like the glitter. I wonder if Charlene was raised here, or if she just landed here because she like the glitter, too."

"Don't ask me. You're the cop," Max said. "I'm the boulevardier and the student of the cocktail. I'm just in this for the giggles. You're in this for that Budweiser tribesman moral imperative that you uptight constable-types seem to thirst for."

They stopped the car near the Loch and got out. Max thought he heard footsteps sounding a few yards away. He stopped. There was no noise now. Lipkin looked at him.

"Thought I heard something," Max said, bending low to scan. "Just my own nerves, I guess."

"Maybe the place is haunted."

Lipkin led the way along the dusty running path. Then he paused by the big oak tree that they both remembered from last night and stepped through the bushes. Sticky yellow tape was wrapped around some of the trees, forming a protected area about eight feet in diameter. The words 'CRIME SCENE – STOP!' were printed on the tape. Here was where Rusty's body had lain.

"You know how I feel about forensic evidence," Lipkin said. "I need as much as I can get. Hair samples and blood are solid, beautiful evidence. I lectured your class about that, didn't I?"

"For hours," Max answered. He heard running steps again but this time much closer. He and Al were back on the jogging path again. He looked up. A hooded clump of runners were coming their way. It looked like a football team running laps at night.

Suddenly, something crashed into Max. He went down heavily and felt a sneaker slam into his face. Another foot kicked him in the back. Suddenly the bushes were filled with bodies.

"Watch it, Al!" he shouted.

"Whoa! Whoa!" the kicker behind him screamed. "Stomping! We going stomping!"

"Look what we got! We got us the police!"

Max rocked to his feet. The football team of runners was on them now. Other kids, howling with the gritty accents of the street – white, black Latino – surrounded him.

Rocks smashed into Lipkin's Cadillac. Lipkin was backed up against his own car, hands held high like a boxer. Four hulking teenagers tried to get at him. He spun and punched one sharply, putting him down, glancing over his shoulder at Max.

"Max!" he shouted. "You're clear! Shoot!"

"We're going stomping!"

Max reached under his jacket and fumbled the Glock out from his holster. "Police officer! Don't move!"

"Shoot!" Lipkin screamed.

Max hesitated. Just then someone slammed into him, and they went down together. He tried to tuck his gun hand under his belly so the mob would not get it. A tangle of feet ran over him and kept kicking. He fought with his free hand and tried to cover up. He smelled the dust of the running feet. Lipkin screamed once, then twice. Max fought to get back to his feet, but there were too many of them on him now. He threw another punch with his free hand. Someone caught the fist. Fingers gouged at his face, trying for his eyes, scraping the skin. He slapped the fingers away, tilted the gun down towards the ground and triggered a shot. The gun bucked.

"Whoa! Gun!"

"Gun! He's shooting!"

Another foot slammed into him. Then they were gone, leaving as quickly and as silently as they had come. Max lay on the ground, panting like a whipped dog, the gun still held in his hand. He tried to get up but he could not. The same running footsteps drummed away into the night. Just a few feet away, he could hear Lipkin weeping quietly.

## CHAPTER 13.

When Max hunched out of the taxi, he could feel the warm New Orleans air break gently over him. He breathed it in deeply and caught the scent of the Mississippi a few blocks away. New Orleans was a steamy tropical city with rich bursts of lush green earth pushing against the gummy sidewalks.

The morning was just starting here. Old black women with knotted bandanas on their heads were slopping water fiercely on the old-fashioned stone steps.

He was wearing a cream colored Pierre Cardin suit with a light blue Oxford shirt, open at the throat. His belt and shoes were made of supple brown leather.

He went under a broad white canopy, leaning heavily on a slim ebony cane with a polished silver head. His left foot dragged. He nodded to a longhaired desk clerk who was watching morning yellow jackets cluster near his steaming coffee cup and made his way painfully up a curling staircase that rose from the lobby. The hotel's garden sang with the bird's waking calls. He threw a look over his shoulder and then knocked softly at a door.

Diana Calia opened the door. She was still in her terrycloth robe, fresh from the shower. Her eyes opened wide, and her head snapped back in surprise, reddish hair falling down onto the robe.

"Max! Is this you? What are you doing in New Orleans?"

"Buying you breakfast. Living life. Doing all those things I couldn't do in New York." He leaned against the doorjamb, breathing hard after his climb. "Recovering."

He was reminded again how lovely she looked. Her eyes were rich and large and blue, holding a critical intelligence that he enjoyed watching. Her hair was tousled and steamy from the shower, giving off its own perfume. She looked like someone with all of life spread out in front of her to enjoy. For the first time in many days, Max felt cheered.

"Why aren't you in the hospital?" she asked. She looked at his battered and bruised face. "How is Sgt. Lipkin?"

"Don't ask. It was my fault. I should have shot some of the little thugs when I had the chance. It won't happen again."

"It wasn't your fault."

"Oh, yes, it was. Who am I going to blame? Their environment?"

She tossed her wet head. "You said the kids were about fifteen years old. Do you want to kill a fifteen-year-old kid who is not even armed? What kind of a man does that?"

"I'd rather have Al healthy and walking around doing what he does than have those hooligans healthy and walking around and doing what they do. That's the trade-off."

She looked at him.

"I still say you weren't to blame."

"Stop it," Max said. "We've been in the hospital for six weeks. Do you know what the term 'stomping' means? A mob of kids goes on a rampage and just destroys everything in their path. Al is all scrambled to hell."

Max's voice turned deeper, almost croaking. Diana had heard that tone before, from plane crash survivors.

"Anyway, never mind all that. You're down here for the same reason I am. There was a schoolboy strangled here last year. You think it might be the same killer who killed the schoolboys in New York?"

"That's right. As I said, the killings are very similar."

"Meanwhile, your poor editor has to pay for this grand hotel deal for you. Look at all this. It's like an Oriental bath."

"He knows how good I am," Diana said with a coy smile.

"That'll do. No more self-promotion, please. I know how you newspaper people are. Time for *le petit dejeuner*."

Max moved carefully past her and picked up the phone to the bed. The bed was in wild disarray. He called room service and ordered rapidly in a low voice as Diana moved out onto her balcony, the sunlight catching her auburn hair.

"Your self-promotion is wasted on me," he added. "I'm not a Daddy Warbucks newspaper publisher with a yacht and yellow necktie to show my power and give you that column. I'm nothing. I'm just a lifeguard in a car wash."

"Better this way," she murmured, coming back inside. "We can talk intimately."

"Powerful word, 'intimately'," he said agreeably.

"I'll tell you another reason I'm in New Orleans," Diana said. "A source at the Manhattan State Psychiatric Hospital phoned me about a woman patient named Charlene who molested boys in New York. She was never arrested. She just drifted in that world that exists between patients, staff and fringe people at any mental hospital. They still gossip about her. She seemed to have a thing against affluent boys."

"So did I," Max said. "Especially when I was growing up around them. They're obnoxious."

"The woman who killed the boy here was named Rosalind," Diana said. "She was a mental patient, too.

Don't you see the connection? What are you doing about it today? Just going to sit around sloshing down booze?"

"You and Al probably have the same source," Max said. "Someone with a grievance and lots of information."

"That's why you and I should solve this together. Please."

"I'm meeting a psychiatrist this afternoon," Max said. "He's an Englishman, Athlstan Shaw, and he seems very reluctant to talk to me."

"Can I sit in?"

"Of course not. He's too shy as it is. Very British. You know, America is a funny country. You self-promote yourselves without a second thought. Reflexively. It is this glad-hander American salesman mentality of the can-do type of fella.

"I remember I was in Mexico once by a poolside in a resort hotel, stretched out in a lawn chair with a few cocktails next to me and reading Lawrence Durrell. All of a sudden this walrus of a fat American salesman type, dressed in watermelon shades of Kmart polyester comes barreling over, suitcases glued to his porky hands. 'I read that book,' he said. 'It's a winner.' 'A winner?' Mister Salesman, go drop dead in a sales conference somewhere. He didn't even know who I was, but he had to pass judgment on the book. Gratuitous. Glib. A can-do type of fella."

"Then why are you here?"

"I'm here because when I was in my hospital bed, I was being tortured by a pair of aging Irish altar boys disguised as NYPD inspectors who wanted to throw me off the job."

Max gazed fondly out at the palm trees and shrubs outside the open window.

"They mumbled very reverently among themselves about what they could do to me. I was becoming a very political football. Luckily, they listened to Al when he said I should be sent down here to investigate."

The clip-clop of a horse's heavy shoes sounded on the street outside. A waiter arrived with their breakfast on a folding table. Smoked kippers, eggs benedict with round humps of Canadian bacon, black glistening Beluga caviar on warm toast and fresh strawberries. They drank from an ice-cold bottle of Veuve-Clicot champagne, Diana filing up her glass like a greedy child playing a grown-up game.

"While I'm in this town," Max said, "think of me as though I'm a freelance. Clear? No aging altar boy supervisors from the Budweiser tribe. No charts or graphs. No fiscal statements." He drank deeply of the champagne. "No regulations about alcohol on my breath."

"I still don't understand how a man like you could be happy as a cop."

"This police mentality is a very interesting and significant phenomenon. There are these thousands of petty rules like you must always wear your uniform hat. You are not to engage in meaningless conversations with the public. You cannot go into a corruption-prone location without your supervisor's permission. Liquor and women are the Devil's traps."

"That's no way to live."

"But the police view mankind as inherently evil. If they do not have all these rules, mankind will run riot and rape and pillage. The cop will drink all day and all night and leap into bed with his neighbor's thirteen-year-old daughter unless his evil nature is restrained. Like the early Christians who used to jump into bed naked with each other. Do you know why?" He drank some more and smiled joyously. "They did it to test their virtue. They felt better after the test. Whether they failed or not."

"Are you going to work this case or just lie around drinking?"

"I'll work hard," he said. "That's why I'm going into the bayou this evening after dark. When strangers can vanish forever. The New Orleans strangler was a woman named Rosalind. No last name."

"The detective assigned to the case heard some street talk that Rosalind was hiding out just south of here in Bayou Lafourche after the killing last year. She may still be there. The detective never had time to look for her. I'll be drinking my way across little tin-hut illegal bars across the bayou, buying drinks, back-slapping and trying to generate some gossip about Rosalind."

"I should go there with you."

"Should you? No chance."

Lulled into a warm glow from the champagne, her slim hands toyed lazily with the robe's sash, as if the right word from Max could coax her to open it and lie down. Her blue eyes caught his. Love affairs had started this way with her before. The touch of fingers on a wine glass, linking them to hands touching, joining gently and both of them spinning safely into a first kiss. But this man Max was slow and shy in his own strange way.

"You're right that I have to keep hard at work," Max said. "And I don't want to keep the Englishman waiting. Being an Englishman means that he has a finer sense of things than we do. He's not a salesman type. He may bugger a little boy at lunchtime but he doesn't go around calling great books 'winners'."

# CHAPTER 14.

Max moved through New Orleans over the next ten days. He met several times with the British psychiatrist, took pages of notes, asked questions about psychopaths and read his notes over and over again. Nobody in Bayou Lafourche south of the city helped him. One bouncer threw him into the street for asking questions.

Learning about psychopaths was frightening. Psychopaths were those who felt no compassion for other people and no sorrow when another person was hurt. They were not connected to others. They believed that fate had dealt the cards and suffering was in the cards. Max knew that his research was oversimplified but he needed to know more about the kind of person that he was hunting.

After his research, Max looked at people on the New Orleans sidewalks and in the bars differently.

He scoured the strange, offbeat bars in the French Quarter, chatting with everyone and leaving good tips. He wanted them to remember him as a buddy. Everyone's pal. There were bikers' bars on Toulouse Street and other dim spots where transvestites bumped gently into tourists. Max felt their long-nailed fingers going over him.

Probing for a gun or a wallet. He was working light and rich. All he had in his pockets was cash.

Max needed the French Quarter as a base. Rosalind, who had murdered a rich boy last year, may have left her mark here. She might still be living close by. Max left Diana in her hotel room so that he could move anonymously and freely through the dark circles of the Quarter. He took a room for himself on Chartres Street.

It was a tired, noisy "rooming hotel" where street people came and went around the clock. Hustlers and con men lived next door to college kids who were saving on expenses in their trip to New Orleans. In the daytime, Max roved through the main library on Loyola Avenue, reading books on psychopathic killers. He met with professors as the Tulane School of Medicine and listened while they told him about serial killers. Jack the Ripper. The Boston Strangler. Richard Speck. David Berkowitz.

"Serial killers are so contradictory, so unknown," Dr. Shaw explained. "They are the modern equivalent of those wandering the roads in the Middle Ages who were thought to be possessed by the Devil. Ted Bundy, the mass murderer, saved dozens of people's lives while he volunteered on a suicide hot line. DeSalvo, the Boston Strangler, was an Army sergeant for nine years.

"It begins in the killer's childhood," he went on. "He or she wants the natural love and bonding most of us get from our parents. And when the father comes home, he might be tired, it might have been a tough day at work or it's too hot to play with his child. So the father spurns him. If this happens not just once or twice, but all the time, the child learns not to expect any sign of love from his parent or from anyone else."

"It can start just from that?" Max asked. "That is enough to have someone slaughtering innocent people twenty years later? It doesn't seem possible."

Dr. Shaw smiled sadly. His fat face was gradually sliding down onto his shirt collar. But his bright eyes stayed young and lively.

"I've seen it in dozens of patients," he said. "Believe me, it can start as humbly as I have described. Have you ever had any children?"

Max scowled. "Everyone's asking me that now. No. I was only married once, and things were a bit too rowdy and roughhouse for me to be siring offspring."

"Starkweather, the thrill killer from Nebraska, was spurned as a baby boy. So was Albert DeSalvo, the Boston Strangler.

Dr. Shaw seemed weighted down by his own sad science as he talked. "The parents had no idea what they doing, of course. None of them were mature enough emotionally to be raising children. But both killers remembered their rejection years later, after they were apprehended for their murders. They documented their rejection and anger at their trials." He threw up his heavy hands. "But nothing changed. The abuse often got worse as the child grows older. Sexual abuse often comes into play, warping the child's own sexual identity."

This information was starting to weigh Max down, too.

"Won't this kind of behavior taper off each year that we learn more about child psychology?" Max asked.

"You may think so," Shaw said. "I don't. Child abuse is more and more common each year. It stays right in step with its finished product of senseless serial killings. This is modern America. You could say that we grow less caring and sympathetic as time goes on. No other country has serial killers the way we do. It seems easier and easier for us to hate and hurt."

℘

Alone in his bare hotel room, Max pored over the notes and paperwork that he was starting to accumulate.

He took sips from a Chivas Regal bottle to help him along. His shadow played on the wall long after midnight while he read and reread his books and NYPD reports.

Serial killers needed to travel. Whoever this killer was, she was able to travel freely. That might be a way to trap her.

Dragging the second victim to death was also a break in pattern. Then a thought struck him. The killer might be experimenting with whatever method gave her the most pleasure. Like a lover deciding what form of lovemaking pleased her the most, the killer could still be dabbling. She could be uncertain how she would kill her next victim.

The idea chilled him and he decided to knock himself out with the bottle. It was too late to go calling on Diana. He did want to do any more solo pub-crawling through the French Quarter tonight. It was exhausting work for him to make the rounds, buy drinks, remember names and listen to stories, hoping to hear something about the killer here.

But nobody seemed to know about Rosalind in New Orleans. They had not heard about a killer preying on the wealthy families. Max was getting discouraged tonight but the whiskey did its work, and he poured himself to sleep.

# CHAPTER 15.

The next day, he breakfasted with a chunky, black-bearded, moon-faced Cajun named Larry Guidroz. He was the NOPD homicide detective assigned to the previous year's strangling of the wealthy private school student.

"Yeah, I think we're looking for the same person," Guidroz agreed. "My victim was a fourteen-year old named Steven Dufrene. A couple of hairs were found under his fingernails. The hair told us that his killer was a black-haired female in excellent physical condition. Maybe a professional athlete, in any case, a very strong girl. The doctors determined that from the protein content. Is your killer in New York a woman?"

"Do you want my opinion or the Department's?"

"Hell with the Department." Guidroz was expansive. "Most departments will screw up a forensics test through ignorance. They don't have the money to keep really good men. The bosses won't spend the money. If they were willing to spend the right way, they could clear up ninety-five percent of their killings, instead of the seventy or seventy-five percent they're doing now."

"That's no surprise. Female hair?"

"I confirmed this by telephone just yesterday. No doubt about it. Our killer is a woman. We found hair on the victim's groin." Max met Guidroz's impenetrable dark eyes. "So I'm convinced. And so is Al Lipkin."

"That's enough for me right there," Guidroz said. "The only reason I'm cooperating with you is because the Superintendent of Police told me to. And Lipkin convinced him over the phone. I gave that Mr. Simmons just what was in the newspapers. Nothing more. But I'll give Lipkin everything I've got because he sounds like one hell of a cop."

"He is."

Guidroz dropped his gravelly voice. "Believe me, I feel bad for Mr. Simmons. But I can't let that scramble my case against this woman, Rosalind. I already told you about her. She was a very violent and aggressive mental patient. Always trying to hurt herself or someone else. This was just before the Dufrene boy was killed. Rosalind used a razor blade she had smuggled into the hospital. She likes razors. She cut up a doctor and escaped from the ward."

"So you think Rosalind could be your strangler? And the New York killer?"

"It's possible," Guidroz said slowly. "From what the doctors told me, she had a lot of anger against wealthy people. She would scream 'Eat the rich!' for hours at a time. That's not necessarily her own slogan. Some of the newer nihilist groups have used that catchy phrase as their own. Rosalind may have just heard it and liked it."

Guidroz rattled his coffee cup before continuing.

"But legitimate causes sometimes pick up nut cases who need to belong to something. Ecologists, anti-abortionists, pro-abortion groups, free choice advocates, every cause. A few splinter groups who are dangerous," Guidroz said. "Especially down here in New Orleans. We got a saying here that if you lift up the United States, everything and everyone that's loose will slide down to New Orleans."

As he got to know the city, Max kept finding out how true that was. He passed through the voodoo shops on Bourbon Street, where mixed-blood Cajuns black priestesses tried to lure tourists inside. The shops were dark pits of mystery away from the strong bright sunlight outside. Inside, they sold charms, statues of voodoo gods, booklets on rituals and potions for the practitioner to use at home.

Max did not shrug the shops off as tourist attractions. He saw that they disturbed the tourists, who would usually find some excuse to go back outside to the sunlight. Something in the shops bothered them. There must have been a reason why voodoo had lasted this long. Brought from West Africa in the hulls of slave ships, mongrel-mixed with Catholic rituals throughout the Caribbean and finally gaining its brightest luster in Haiti, despite the government's 300-year struggle against the religion. Voodoo had survived all that fervor against it and now reigned supreme in dark and hushed spots around the world.

༄

Max often had breakfast with Diana in her hotel room after he had been going through the bars all night, making friends and throwing down tips while he was listening for talk about his killer. His stomach usually churning, he needed the fresh air on her patio.

"Why do you guys drink so much?" she asked one morning. "You're a gifted, intelligent man. It must mean something special, something that I don't understand. What does it mean to you?"

"Drinking is just drinking to me. No, maybe that isn't true," he corrected himself. "I'm no street person. Too bookish and complex. But for some street people, liquor is all that they have. With drinking, they can be anyone and do anything. Instead of what they really are. And liquor is the only thing that frees them. They can soar, talk differently and behave wildly, using the booze like a kid uses a playground. Drinking heavily is risky and exciting because nobody knows what will happen. All the other parts of their life are rigid. They know what will happen."

"This is such a long shot," she said. "You're roaming everywhere to catch this killer. There are so many women in this country. And so much anger."

"And so many angry women," he said.

He caught a glimpse of her fresh young face against the morning sunlight and thought about his wife again. He hummed his bit of song absentmindedly as Diana served him a hot croissant.

"Your trip down here is an expensive gamble," Diana sounded like she was scolding him. "Does the Department have that kind of money? What are you trying to do?"

"Ohhh, I don't know," Max massaged his throbbing temples with his fingertips. "Maybe to beat the Budweiser tribe at this detective game. Hear this, Lady Diana. I am not a detective. Never have been and never will be. The Department put me in a blue uniform and will never, ever take me out of it. I am a misfit. I will never fit in. Never wear yellow power neckties, a positive confident smile or go around calling books 'winners'."

"I'd like to know where you get all your damn money," Diana said. "You're throwing down cash like the last of the French Quarter high-rollers. The Department must really want this one solved. Is Lipkin that respected?"

"Among the few that know, yes. You can't recruit a man like Al. He can do so many things so well – crime scene searches, interviewing witnesses, forensics and autopsy reports, managing the different personalities, teaching the rookie detectives that the Department just has to keep him stimulated. He could make so much money in business, with his mind and talent."

"It's more than that. There's something that you're not telling me. No cop ever spent money like this before."

"And they never will again."

"I'm being kept in the dark here. Something's not right."

She stood up from the sofa and began to pace.

"Meanwhile, this crusade is wrecking what was left of your health. Your body is trying to recover from the shock of your injuries, and you're drinking straight whiskey every time I turn around. You know you're getting a gut on you now?"

Max waved a thick hand at the breakfast cast and smiled. "It's from this rich food and the many fine cocktails that I enjoy while in the illustrious company of tosspots and publicans."

"You better hope you win this game. Do you know what it's costing you?"

## CHAPTER 16.

Mornings started slowly and painfully for Lipkin. Usually he would awaken, half-hoping that his pains had stopped sometime during the night and then realized that they were still there.

But this morning was different: he had visitors. Wendell Simmons, Rusty's father, came to his hospital room folding a bulky tan trench coat and shaking his head. Watching him, Lipkin realized suddenly that it had been raining all morning. With Simmons was a woman. She was much younger than he, with a short stylish haircut and thick eyeglasses.

"I hope that we're not waking you up, Sergeant," Simmons said. "The floor nurse said you had been up for hours."

"The name is 'Al'," Limpkin said, sitting up. "In here, I'm damn sure not a sergeant. Just 'Al' is fine."

"I would hate to disturb your sleep."

Lipkin sensed that Simmons wanted to be asked about his own state of mind.

"How's your sleep?" he asked. "Are you getting enough?"

"I keep having nightmares. Which is natural, I guess. I keep seeing Rusty running along that bridle path. Over and over again. But Dr. Soren is prescribing some sedatives for me, and they help."

"I'm glad to hear that. Soren is your family doctor?"

"No." The woman spoke up for the first time. "He's a psychiatrist."

Lipkin recognized the woman by her soft, timid voice. She was one of Rusty's teachers, the one who had cried.

"We've met before, I think," he said.

"Yes. I'm Miss Sangster." She was handling her own raincoat, a black vinyl New Age styled belted one. "You came to the school with that other officer. I was so sorry to hear that you had been hurt."

"I've been hurt worse before," Lipkin lied, thinking it was a stupid thing to say. "But I'll be around better soon."

Lipkin realized that it must be later than he thought. Visiting hours started at 11:00 a.m. Lipkin knew that well. It was, along with his meal times, one of the few set rules in his current life.

Simmons was talking again.

"I just stepped in to see how you were and to see if there's anything I can do to make sure you're comfortable. I'm afraid that like a lot of New Yorkers, I used to take the police for granted because I had never needed them. When I did need you, you were –" his voice hesitated, searching for the right words, "– very good to me. Your partner, also."

"Max is one in a million."

"Which doctor is looking after you?" Miss Sangster asked.

"That's a good point, Lily," Simmons said. "There might be something we can do about that."

"Please, no, Mr. Simmons." Lipkin grinned shakily, his stiff gray whiskers sharp against his pale skin. "No Viennese specialists. I'm getting all the attention I need. The

Cardinal has been in to see me, even though I'm Jewish, and the Channel Four News crew will be doing a bedside interview with me."

"But I keep seeing him running," Simmons repeated. "He didn't like to run. I made him do it."

"That killer was going to kill somebody," Lipkin said bluntly. "D'you hear me? Rusty just happened to be in the wrong place at the wrong time. You can't spend the rest of your life regretting the fact that he was out running that night. You're the one this happened to. If it wasn't you, it would have been some other innocent family suffering."

Simmons looked down at his hands, locked tightly together.

"This is the worst pain in the world," he said. "When I lost my wife to leukemia, I thought that nothing could be worse. But this is." He sighed, shook his head and got to his feet. "I've got to make a phone call, Al. There's one down the hall. I'll be right back."

"You can use this phone here. The city is paying for it."

"No, no. This may take a moment or two. I'll be back," Simmons said, closing the door behind him.

Lily looked at Lipkin.

"He's calling Suzanne," she said. " Or Roshi. Or one of the other women he spends time with. He's told me about them. The conversations he has with them. They're strange conversations. Disturbing. That's why he didn't want to use this phone."

"How do you know all this?"

"He talks freely when he's drinking. And he's always drinking now. I think they're from an escort service."

Lipkin shrugged. "I guess he can afford it. Have you met any of the women? How do they strike you?"

"Manipulative. But it's harmless. Like you say, he can afford it." She changed the subject. "How many visitors do you get in here?"

"Not many, besides cops."

"Any girlfriends or wives?" she asked, grinning playfully.

"I'm twice-divorced. I call then 'W-One' and 'W-Two.' Like World War I and World War II. They're not likely to visit. They're more likely to hire another gang to come in here and finish the job."

"You should be dating someone then." She smiled. "Just to feel alive."

"Ms. Sangster, I should not be dating. Like an old infantryman, I've got thirty years on the line. Twice captured by the enemy. Tortured, grievously wounded and I barely escaped with my life. You want me to start that whole mess all over again? I feel alive enough right now, thank you very much."

"All right, then, Sergeant. You've almost convinced me that you're telling the truth. But only almost. So I'll be around to visit you."

"You're just making talk. You don't want to see me."

"You don't think so?" she smiled widely. "You don't know much about women."

When Simmons returned, he seemed calmer and more collected than before. "I see you're still working on this case from your bed, Al." He pointed to the messy stack of NYPD reports and psychology textbooks on the bedside table. "The signs of a workaholic? I've recognized that quality in some of my employees. You should watch that."

"I always tell myself I'll watch it on the next case."

Lipkin noticed that Simmons' color had changed as well as his demeanor. He had probably taken a pill to alter his mood when he had left the room, Lipkin decided.

"We'll be on our way now, Al. You have my home telephone number," Siinmons said. "Please feel free to call me if there's anything I can do to help."

Lily held out her hand and shook hands with Lipkin "You'll let me come back to visit you, Al?" she asked. "You won't turn into an uptight policeman and chase me away?"

"Chase you away?" Lipkin grinned. "You don't know much about men."

## CHAPTER 17.

A Spanish flamenco dancer named Manuel sometimes played at sunset in Jackson Square. He sang under the high stone arches of the Cabildo Theater, a handsome monument dating back to the time the French had owned New Orleans.

Manuel's songs were gypsy songs from the south of Spain, crying out to the moon in the season of the wine harvest, Manuel's lover, a slim blonde girl, danced and shook the tambourine as he sang his songs. Max had met them both in the saloons. They had swapped lies about their travels in Spain.

Tonight was a good night for the money. So when Manuel caught sight of Max crossing the square, he called for him to come over. The last song was just ending. The three of them began a night of drinking. Maria, the blonde girl, had a feather boa, under which was a bottle filled with some kind of fiery dark wine. They drank freely under the Cabildo's arches in the fading gray light.

A blond-bearded horse-and-buggy driver named Ben joined them and agreed to take a few pulls from the bottle. Ben was one of the original hippies. His Irish face made him look like a mischievous fairy-sprite in the twilight.

Together they drained the bottle and then trooped over to them Toulouse Street Cinema where New Orleans's smallest coziest bar did a lazy, slow kind of business.

There were only four stools in the Toulouse Street Cinema cafe and a meager selection of drinks. Ben said it was like drinking inside your father's private study, where you knew how everything would taste and how you would feel. For these four travelers, each a long way from home, the cafe felt like home.

The bartender, who was also the projectionist and the ticket-ticker, served them glasses of wine. He had originally intended to use these four stools for the theatergoers at intermissions and after the show. He had not wanted to run a saloon.

This cinema showed vintage classics. Movies like *The Manchurian Candidate*, *Teorema*, *Wasp Woman*, *The Passenger* and other cult favorites. New Orleans was starved for these old films, and the young people in the Quarter always came to the theater in black leather packs.

The crowd from the six o'clock show broke like a wave over the theater and then settled into their seats. The bartender left Max and his friends alone, on the honor system. Manuel was talking about Spain when he mentioned a woman who had vacationed there. Her name was Rosalind. She had appreciated Manuel's songs as part of the Spanish culture.

"I think I met her, too," Max said carelessly, the pulse in his throat thumping all of a sudden. "Where is she now?"

"I'm not sure." Manuel had a dark face, mottled with a constant sunburn from playing outdoors. His dark eyes were always merry, especially when he was drinking. "She used to live in a rooming house on Conti Street," he said. "Maybe she's back there."

The bartender returned, and Max threw down some money to buy another round. He waited for a few minutes and then asked Manuel what Rosalind had looked like.

"Oh, like before, when she was living in the Quarter."

"Did she drop out of sight?" Max asked.

"I didn't see her around last year."

Max nodded to himself. That fit. Rosalind had been in the Hotel Dieu Hospital and fled into Bayou Lafourche. Max had spent a hot, dangerous afternoon looking for her. But she was long gone.

"She looks different?"

"You know. She's still got the red hair. But it's cut short in punk style now. She's still wearing black."

"Black boots?"

"I don't remember. Maybe."

"That might the same Rosalind I knew. I owe her some money from the last time we were out bouncing through the cafes here. Is she working anywhere?"

"You know that Rosalind doesn't work. It's strange that you knew her, Max. She seemed pretty unhappy most of the time."

"Hell, I used to know everybody in the Quarter." Max paused. "Where on Conti Street is that rooming house? I know one near Bourbon Street."

"No, closer to here. Closer to the river. Just a block or two from here."

Max turned to other topics and then began talking with Maria, Manuel's lover. She was a blonde, fresh-faced girl from Minnesota, long-waisted and graceful in the Mexican peasant dress that she wore tonight. It was always easy and refreshing to talk with Maria. She had the knack of finding the cheerful part of whatever happened. A lot of street people in the Quarter lived that way. They needed the attitude and clung to it in order to survive.

Max went to the pay phone outside the Cinema entrance and dialed Larry Guidroz at the New Orleans Homicide Squad office.

The detective who answered said that Guidroz was off duty for the next two days and they would not give out his home number. Max left the message about Rosalind's whereabouts and supplied his own number for Guidroz. The detective said he would do what he could.

Max went back inside to get his last drink for a while. Ben brought him a glass of Rossi burgundy and watched as Max tipped the bartender heavily.

"We've got to keep in touch, the four of us," Max said. "You know that I've been looking at real estate here in the Quarter. I may have found a house that I want to buy, over near Jean Lafitte's old blacksmith shop."

"That's gonna cost you lots of jack," Ben whistled.

"Once this inheritance jive is settled, I got lots of jack," Max lied, wishing it were true. "But I won't be able to stay in the house all the time. Have to hit Europe and South America to tie up some more family business. So I'll need some good friends to house-sit for me while I'm away."

He knew this would interest them. Housing was their biggest expense.

"Somebody I can trust," Max lied, leading them on.

"Whatever we can do for you," Manuel's Castilian accent was growing thicker with the wine. "That is no problem."

"None whatsoever," Maria smiled whitely, nodding her blonde head.

Ten o'clock found Max standing near the only rooming house on Conti Street. He had walked the street up and down, peering at the old iron doorways, checking for cards in the windows and examining the buzzers for the signs of a rooming house.

He had spoken with cab drivers, cops and local residents to make sure that this was the only rooming house on Conti Street. Rosalind might be living here.

The building was old-fashioned and set back off the sidewalk. A wrought-iron gate blocked the way into a small courtyard. Max could see it from the street. There were probably a dozen cubicles upstairs, holding a dozen different tenants who paid by the week. New Orleans was the crossroads of America. Everybody passed through it at one time or another but only a few stayed more than six months. It was like Key West, Greenwich Village or Santa Monica in that way. Tourists landed to see what it was like and then moved on. French Quarter people rented everything: rooms, television sets, furniture and work tools.

It was a close, muggy night like so many others in this city. The scent of the Mississippi River hung over the dark streets. Here and there along the block, shoe leather quietly scraped concrete. But for the most part, the block grew quieter as the night dragged on. Cars did not come into the Quarter on some nights. Every so often, a horse-drawn buggy would clop past, the driver heading wearily back to the stables on Esplanade Avenue, after a night of ferrying tourists around.

Max was smoking a Macanudo cigar studiously and quietly, drawing on the rolled green leaf and sending smoke up to the cloudy sky. He was also taking occasional pulls on the hip flask he had remembered to fill with Chivas.

He needed some way to pass the time and still keep an eye on the building. He was not a cop in New Orleans and had no police authority. Just a tourist on a public street, getting himself slightly drunk.

There would be no Budweiser tribesmen from the NYPD to come along and suspiciously smell his breath. No Lieutenant Quinnliven to solemnly bring him up on Departmental charges for Conduct-Unbecoming-An-Officer.

He stayed there until his watch told him it was 4:00 a.m. Either Rosalind stayed in her cubicle that night, or she was bedded down somewhere else. Anyway, he was exhausted and out of whisky.

He limped the few blocks to his own bed, set the alarm and stretched out to get a few hours of fast sleep.

# CHAPTER 18.

At eight the next morning, he got up and dressed in his surveillance clothes: dark blue T-shirt, black cotton windbreaker, blue baseball cap, sunglasses, comfortable faded blue jeans and Reebok running shoes. He might have to do some running after Rosalind. He had a photocopy of the warrant Detective Guidroz had shown him, authorizing any cop in Louisiana to arrest Rosalind on Escape-From-Confinement. He filled up his flask again and loaded his pockets with cash, travelers cheques and cigars. He had no weapon and no police shield. He was working light and rich, as usual.

Two cups of Cafe Du Monde chicory coffee helped snap him awake. He wolfed down hot blueberry and apple turnovers, feeling better as the sugar hit his system. Then he telephoned Guidroz's office and got another homicide man, who told him that Guidroz was still off duty and not expected to call in. Max patiently left a second message.

He could not put more pressure on to catch Rosalind without alienating Guidroz or embarrassing him. Cops were very touchy that way.

Even at this early hour, Max was sweating. He could feel the New Orleans heat slithering like a snake through the streets of the Quarter.

Early morning tourists were trooping down the street now, the way home from the bars and wearing hats from the Pat O'Brien's Famous Hurricane Bar. They whooped and staggered over the flagstones, calling drunkenly to each other.

"Don't they ever close the bars in this town?" a woman asked her husband in a flat Midwestern twang as they hobbled past Max.

"Don't have to," he answered in the same nasal accent. "In New Orleans, every night is Saturday night, and every Saturday night is New Year's Eve."

Max stayed at his stakeout, watching the house until the noon whistle blew. A few tenants came out, shaking their heads and scratching themselves. Max wondered idly how many other serial killers were waking in the Quarter this very same morning.

With dozens of active killers in this country, he figured there had to be a few others drawn to the wildness, the bright colors and abundance of transients the Quarter offered.

He pressed the bell, his pulse and temples pounding. No answer. He decided it was time to go inside. He pressed the bell again.

He knew Rosalind might answer. He had nothing to protect himself with. His cane was back at his hotel. It was hard to follow someone unnoticed with a cane in your hand.

The woman who came down the staircase was huge and pale, with mounds of wrinkled pink skin crammed into a tight blue housedress. The steps squeaked under her weight. Her scanty gray and pinkish hair was pulled under a sunbonnet.

"Yeah?" she grunted, a woman who looked like she had seen it all.

"I'm looking for a room," Max said. "Do you have any?"

The gate swung open. The woman reached out a big freckled arm that looked like loose dough and waved Max inside.

"The place I'm staying in right now is dreadful, absolutely dreadful," Max prattled on truthfully. "I had no idea I would be in such a déclassé establishment while visiting New Orleans on a business trip. And there's so much riff-raff in the streets. I hope that you always keep this gate locked."

"Each tenant gets his own key for the gate. Five dollar deposit," she wheezed. "Then you get a room key. Five-dollar deposit. You not allowed hot plates in the rooms."

As she brought Max back upstairs, they passed by old wooden doors with numbers hastily scratched into the wood, 7, 4 and 3. They were all closed.

"Do you have showers?"

"We got one john for the men and one for the girls. Each one separate. That's a dollar extra per week. No guests allowed in here after ten pee-em during the week and midnight on the weekend."

"Could I see one of the rooms? Just for a quick look inside." Max started reaching into the pocket of his jeans.

"Let's see who's up. Bubba's gone to work. So's Mister Arthur. I guess you can take a look there, real quick."

The door to one room opened up into the hallway and Max nearly jumped from nervousness. But it was a scrawny-looking young girl with wet blonde hair, not fitting Rosalind's description. There was still soap on her thin neck as she came into the hall, toweling herself dry.

"Morning, Miss Ellen," the landlady said.

"Who's this?" she asked sharply, looking at Max. Max attempted a cheery smile.

"Gentleman's looking to rent a room soon as we get a vacancy.

"Sure he is."

"I am," Max said. "I think a friend of mine stayed here once. Miss Rosalind. Lady with red hair?"

The landlady nodded. The blonde girl hooted.

"Sure, you're gonna live here!" the blonde girl said. "Looking for Rosalind? You pimp motherfucker. That's why you were outside all last night? Waiting for her? You cheap pimp! You were right under my window." Her voice carried. Doors unlatched along the hall.

"He was?" the landlady asked. "Mister, why you lying to me here? What are you doing, in my house? ROSALIND! ROSALIND! Who is this man, honey?"

Before Max could do anything, one of the doors down the hall opened and a hefty woman with spiky red hair came out. She wore black clothing and took in the group at a glance.

"Rosalind, what you up to —" the landlady said just as Max started to move forward. She slammed Max back against the flimsy wall and his back screamed with pain. "You stay put, mister. Rosalind —"

Max slipped and fell to the floor, on his hands and knees. The blonde swung a basketball sneaker into his ribs to knock him down again.

"Get back," he panted. "I'm a police officer."

"Pimp is what you are!"

The blonde girl swung for his groin and missed. Rosalind started running for the stairs.

"You a police, where's your badge? C'mon, where?" The landlady shouted, grabbing Max's forearm. He shook her loose, tempted to slug her. Rosalind's feet made noises on the stairs.

Max was bounding down the steps after her. But she was already out and running on Conti Street. She was a good thirty feet ahead, racing over the flagstones. His heart jumped against his bruised ribs.

"Pimp motherfucker! Pimp!" the blonde girl shouted, running behind Max. A cheap pocketknife in her hand glinted in the strong morning sun. "I'll cut the nuts off of you!"

# CHAPTER 19.

Rosalind ran onto Jackson Square, scattering pigeons and tourists in the noontime crowd. Her feet made fast smacking sounds over the stones. Max lurched, coughed and wheezed his way after her. There were no cops on the street. The line of cars blocked him until he threaded his steps around them. Rosalind was getting farther away. And the blonde girl with the knife was still screaming close behind him about what she would do.

"Lucky dogs!" a hot dog vendor hollered, holding up a pink one on his fork. "I got lucky dogs here! Get them while they're hot, yeah!"

"Police!" Max bellowed just as loud. "Police officer! Stop that woman! She's wanted by the police!"

The crowd kept watching. Nobody made a move to stop Rosalind as she ran past the flower boxes filled with magnolias and onto Decatur Street. Cars honked and slammed on their brakes.

Beyond the traffic, there were the railroad tracks and the wide Mississippi River.

"Call the police!" Max roared. "She killed someone."

He ran some more.

"Fuck due process right now," he said under his breath. "We need a lynch mob."

Rosalind weaved her way through the horse-drawn carts and the screaming horns and reached the other side of Decatur Street.

She ran up the asphalt walk that went over the railroad tracks.

Max followed the black clothing as she ran furiously, her legs pumping. He blocked out everything else and concentrated on moving forward, as fast as he could, hurtling after her, leaping over the railroad tracks and feeling the ties stub his toes. His breath thinned out again. He sucked great gulps of air down into his lungs, trying to get his second wind.

Tourists scattered around him in eddies as he rocketed past them, their surprised faces and yips of alarm.

The riverbank walk along the Mississippi was crowded with tourists. Max looked wildly around for a uniform NOPD shirt but did not see any. Rosalind was fleeing west now, into the area filled with railway yards and coffee warehouses. She could hide there easily and make her escape. Max would never see her again.

He put on a burst of speed and closed the gap, feeling the pain from his wounds corkscrew through him. His legs felt like stone. Finally, he managed to kick out at one of her ankles.

He missed. She threw a look over her shoulder, lips skinned furiously. He tried again. This time his toe spun her off balance, and she went down in a heap.

Max breathed out, relieved, but she came roaring to her feet again, bellowing in a man's voice and slugged Max across the face. Blood spurted onto his shirt. Then she hit him backhand. Something sliced into his skin. He could feel it slice. His skin gave way like a ripe plum's.

She had something in her hand. Max backpedaled furiously, coughing and racking up breath from the run. Her hand skidded off his throat. She was trying for his throat. He was too tired to block.

"Somebody help me!" He raped me!" Rosalind screeched like a bobcat. "He's trying to kill me! Won't somebody help me!"

Max missed a lunge and crashed into an old man on the crowded levee boardwalk. The man, dressed in tourist clothing, righted himself and pushed Max away. Their eyes met.

"Call the police," Max said clearly, watching Rosalind. "Call 911."

"What for?"

Rosalind slammed into Max again, and he toppled to the boardwalk. She kicked and her boot came away bloody. Max howled, fending off another kick.

But he rolled to his feet, shuffled once under her wild swing and threw a fist into her stomach. She blew out breath and sagged. Feet sounded on the levee behind him.

Max was bleeding freely now, blood spatters falling like crimson coins.

"Yeah, we can help!" someone shouted behind him.

"About time," Max muttered.

"Go for it!"

Something smashed into his back, staggering him. He smelled beer and turned painfully to see the excited pink faces, flushing with beer and nerve up for a free fight. The tourists were looking for some fun in colorful old New Orleans. One wrestled Max down while another tried out punches on his gut. A third guy tried to kick him. Rosalind was getting to her feet again after the belly punch. Max saw the glitter of a razor blade between her fingers.

"Watch out!" Max cried. "She's got a razor! She's gonna cut you, bro!"

The puncher turned his head. Max kicked him in the shin and stomped down on his foot. The tourists saw Rosalind's razor and skittered backwards. Max stepped forward, freed one arm and elbowed the tourist in the jaw. The one trying to kick him connected with a foot to Max's groin, whooping wildly as Max crumpled.

"Whoo! Party! Party!" the tourist yelled. "Go for it!"

Max rolled, trying to cover up and stopped when somebody's leg blocked him. It was the old man who was still standing there, watching.

"I'm going to call the police," Max heard him say slowly, regretfully. "I can't believe that this is an authorized type of arrest here. This is not the way to do it. I'm going to call."

"Good idea," Max mumbled as someone else kicked him, jarring his head against the ground. It rocked him. His cheek scraped. When he looked up again, the levee was full of police uniforms and growling radio noises.

"Everybody just stand still!" the lead cop was shouting, a big nickel-plated Magnum in his hand. "First joker pisses me off gets whipped! Stand still!"

Rosalind was standing, her hands wet with Max's blood. She was screaming like the rest of them.

"Officer!" Max shouted. "New York Police!"

"Thought I told you to hush!" the cop shouted.

"Murder warrant on that woman!" Max said. "Detective Guidroz from your Homicide Squad wants her. Be careful. She's got a razor."

A beefy sergeant in a uniform blouse that was too tight spun Rosalind around in an arm-lock, put her on a knee and speed- cuffed with her hands in back.

"She ain't got nothing now," he said.

# CHAPTER 20.

Max remembered the worst hangover he had ever had in his life. When his heart and head had kept pounding in a sickening, nonstop rush, and he suffered through the dry heaves. This was worse.

"I wasn't much help," Diana said. She was standing next to the bed in her hotel room.

"This isn't *The Thin Man* and you're not Nora Charles," he said. "No reason for you to mess in this foolishness."

"You're going to have two scars across your cheek. Even after they heal and close up, they're going to show. The doctor told me that. I turned him upside down about the shape you're in. You can heal better in my room here than in that filthy hospital."

"Listen, my dear reporter, I don't care about the scars. Women are just going to have to overlook my scars the same way they have to forgive my other defects. My days of modeling swimwear for Brooks Brothers are long past. I can lie here and sling wisecracks up to the sky all day long if you're going to keep giving me such good material."

She shook her head and moved restlessly to the other end of the room. "The doctor said you should still be resting after your injuries, after that other attack," she said. "You could kill yourself this way. You had the blood pressure of an 'exhausted street drunk' was the way he put it. Not enough food and way too much alcohol."

"An exhausted street drunk," he mused. "That's one way to describe a boulevardier, I suppose." He lightly touched the bandages along his face. "My ribs are taped, too. Something broken there from a kick."

"Fractured cheekbone. Scalp laceration, possible fractured skill, new bruises on top of old ones."

The door opened and Larry Guidroz came inside, breathing quickly through his mouth like some kind of prize steer. His lightweight tropical clothes looked like he had slept in them.

"Royster, you through here, boy!" he shouted. "You are history around, Bubba! Soon as you can walk, you walking out of my city."

Max recognized the signs of a passionate cop, barely in control of himself. Guidroz was seething. His thick hands opened and closed. The thick, hot-blooded temper of the Cajuns who intermarried with Canary Islanders with Spanish names like Guidroz and Perez showed in his flushed face.

"You said you wouldn't embarrass me!" Guidroz shouted. "Motherfucker this bullshit! Y'all turn the Quarter upside down, cause a riot in Jackson Square, and get some drunk-ass tourists nearly killed by us police. I just left the Superintendent's office, and he tore me a new asshole. I'll be lucky to stay on the Homicide Squad behind this bullshit. If I get bounced, y'all watch out, that's all I can say."

"Larry, calm down," Max said, nodding to Diana. "Meet my friend, Diana. She's a reporter."

Guidroz looked like his worst nightmares were coming true. His pale eyes opened to scrutinize Diana. She was wearing a black sheath cocktail dress that made her look as rare and lovely as an exotic wildflower. She had dressed to cheer Max up by reminding him of cabaret women and how they adorned themselves. Guidroz saw her hand holding Max's. He also saw there was no wedding ring.

"There's not going to be any embarrassment, Larry," Max said. "The Super's only making noise."

"Yeah, but he's making it at me. And he's my Super." He sputtered. "What's she doing here? Who is she?"

"*New York Daily News*. Diana Calia," she said, extending her free hand.

"New York? Oh, Je-sus!"

No civilian could understand Guidroz's dread right now. He had been punished and wounded by his commanding officer in the NOPD's paramilitary structure. He had just blown his cool and revealed his secrets to an outsider, a beautiful unattached Yankee reporter. She might report everything he said.

"Larry, I know how you feel. Your bosses can't hurt me, so they'll settle for hurting you. Cop bosses are all the same that way. But they'll cool down, partner. I promise you. You did clear up a murder case, your schoolboy strangling."

"I didn't clear up nothing," Guidroz replied. "Pascagoula, Mississippi PD had Rosalind in their jail for disorderly conduct on the same day Stephen Dufrene was strangled. The booking slip was in her papers at her room. I called the chief in Pascagoula to verify it myself. They fingerprinted her on the ten-day drunk charge but never sent the prints out of state. Why would they send them? They didn't know she was a murder suspect."

"She didn't kill Stephen," Max said. "Who did?"

"It don't matter," Guidroz answered. "The bosses are screaming for my head right now. You think I should remind them that I can't close out that case? Like hell I will. Right now, I stay out of sight and keep them calm. You know. You used to be a cop."

"Max?" Diana spoke for the first time. "What's this? What does it mean, 'you used to be a cop'?"

Guidroz shot her a quick, piercing look.

"What is this?" She was building up steam. "You have been stringing me along."

"Hold on, Miss Daily News," Guidroz said. "I'm not through with his ass yet. You can have what's left. Max, it might help if I can tell my boss you've gone back to New York. That you're not in the Quarter anymore, planning any more stunts like this. Tell me that. Tell me you're leaving just as soon as you can fucking travel."

"Tell them that, Larry, yeah. If they press you, tell them that. Don't volunteer it. But if my going away can help you, I'm gone. And I'm very sorry to get you jammed up like this. I wish they could hit me instead of you, Larry. I'm the guy that deserves it."

Guidroz nodded gruffly and strode from the hospital room, still angry.

Max looked over at Diana's hot, excited blue eyes and closed his own wearily.

"Everyone's furious with me," he said. "Things were easier when I was asleep. This isn't like the movies when the wounded hero wakes up and everyone cheers."

"What are you playing at?"

"Why, oh why, can't life be more like the movies?"

Sometimes during the night, Max woke up. The suite was dead quiet. His back throbbed with thick pain where the kicks had landed.

Diana was seated on the balcony with the door open, six feet away. Her eyes held him as he rose up. "Are you all right?" she asked.

"Hurting some." His mouth was dry.

She was wearing her white terrycloth robe. Newspapers were spread out over the balcony's table. She had been reading them all night, poring over various articles. The French Quarter lay silent. The bars were closed.

"I was just admiring you," she said huskily. "Looking at your face while you slept. You looked so calm. And then, as if somebody waved a wand, you woke up like a little kid. Scrunched up your face and tightened your whole body."

Max blew out a breath. Then he raised his battered head and touched his bruised skin.

As she loomed over him, Max reached up, gently opened the robe's sash and put his mouth on her breast. His strong arms came up around her back, hugging her to him. The robe opened, showing her secret skin, the body he had never seen before. He had not touched her before this.

"Ohhh, yes!" Diana said, breaking down on top of him. His mouth moved her to surrender. Hotly and suddenly, she let him remove her robe.

He felt her lean runner's body with delight, savoring her skin and holding her tightly. He slithered out of his boxer shorts and felt her hands moving down his scarred thigh.

His own beaten body cried out against moving but he ignored it. Then her sweet weight was on him, grounding him safely onto the bed.

This was what they had both been waiting for, both been dancing around with the looks and the casual touches and closeness and danger, waiting for the right moment.

# CHAPTER 21.

Max slept deeply in the soft hotel bed while Diana camped out on the sofa, surrounded by his textbooks, writing a 700-word piece on the New Orleans killing. She gazed at him while he slept.

"Why do you never talk about your wife, Max?" she asked when he awoke. "I think that's a bad sign."

"Do you now? Well, that's penetrating of you."

"But I want to know." She grinned impishly, but he knew that she was serious. "I have a right to know. Can't you see that?"

"I can see I'll get no peace until I talk," Max answered. "We met while I was running a boxing gym and teaching English in Guanajuanto, Mexico. One of my friends was a Texan who worked out in the gym. His family came to visit him and I met his sister, Lisa.

"Guanajuanto is one of the most beautiful places I have ever seen," he went on. "The Spanish built it in the 16th century, using all the gold and silver plundered from the Aztecs. It's a city of gold and silver, built alongside a mountain with underground cobblestone streets that crisscross under the mountain."

"I should have seen trouble coming that night," he said. "They were so much a family, so much a clan. And I was loose and friendly with them, thinking their down-home Texas talk was a novelty. Then his sister, this woman, took my breath away. I fell for her right away. I had shipped out around the world and worked all over so I was an experienced thirty-six-year-old. She was only twenty-three. So I asked her to stay with me in Guanajuanto."

"She should have laughed at you," Diana smiled graciously. "That's what I would have done."

"She looked at me aghast. Be the lover of an aging, paunchy adventurer who lived over a Mexican boxing gym?" Max threw back his head and laughed joyously. "She 'demurred', is the right word. She and her family left the next day. But the lights stayed on all night in my room. For the first time, their buzzing bothered me."

Max drove a fist into his open palm.

"Guanajuanto bothered me. The silver and gold-crusted streets. I knew it was time to take a chance. So I borrowed a jeep and started bouncing my way through the desert towards the border. I kept remembering how she had looked.

"The jeep died. I sold it to a gas station dealer and started hitchhiking, watching the Gila monsters and rattlers come up onto the roadway while I was standing there with my thumb out. There were no buses. And I was in a hurry. Finally, I made it over the border and into Texas. I found her reading on her porch at sundown."

"So far all your talk about her," Diana said, somewhat defensively, "has been about you. That's the trouble with you 'adventurers.' You're all little boys. You like the adventure of marrying but not marriage itself. What was SHE like? Does she even have a name?"

"Lisa. Talented, inventive, loving fascinating. I wanted to show her all the beauties of different places. Both of us had the same skills. We could cook or teach anywhere. Live comfortably while working in either Mexico or Asia. So we compromised and settled on New Orleans."

"Here?" Diana asked. "New Orleans?"

"Gateway city to the great Southwest," Max said. "The Southwest starts here, in my view. We lived here for a while and then went on to New Mexico, Arizona and Texas. Then New York and Florida. Depression hit her. She missed Texas and her family and started drinking more. And then back to New York for a painful time."

His voice dipped.

"I don't remember much from that time. I blocked it, the marriage counselor said. All of me was concentrated on Lisa. Nothing else mattered."

He dropped his bruised head, his mouth drawn downwards.

"Her family had split apart. They could not stand to be near each other. That broke her up. She's drifting somewhere through Texas now, drinking all that she can hold. She's bloated and ugly from what she's done to herself."

A carriage went by in the French Quarter Street outside.

"I guess you did live down here in New Orleans," she said. "Seriously now, did you?"

"I wouldn't call it living," Max said. Telling his story seemed to have drained him. He rocked forward and a lock of red hair fell down against his scarred cheek.

"You must have been impossible to live with," she said. "All that traveling around, loose-footed, all that going where you wanted."

Max said nothing.

"Women want different things than men do," she continued. "We see things differently, especially as we get older."

"I'm going to sleep some more."

"But I want to talk about this."

"I'm going to sleep," Max said. "If I can. If you didn't open a blue jug of nightmares with your curiosity."

He turned away from her, his wild hair playing out over the pillow.

He woke up some time later and watched Diana come in from the balcony. She had been reading her newspapers there again.

"If you're not a cop, who's bankrolling you?" Diana asked. "Where is the money coming from?"

"I think I've had enough moving around. Time for me to go back to beddy-bye."

"Dammit, that's my beddy-bye you're wallowing in like a hippo. Are you a cop or not? Yes or no?"

"I've got my own room a few blocks from here," Max reminded her.

"I'd like to see you get there tonight. Come on, Max, I feel like you're taking advantage of me. How can you be so calculating?"

"You should see the guys I work for."

"Are you still a cop? Let's start there."

"Let's start tomorrow. I'm still wounded, remember?"

"You have to tell me."

"Do I? That must be a new rule," he said in his deep schoolteacher's voice. "I figured that unless I'm on the Department rolls I don't have to obey any of those three thousand persnickety pettifroggery Irish commandments. So if I'm to have any peace, let's you and I go off the record now. Is that a deal?"

She nodded, too casually.

"Please indulge me, Lady Diana. Say that we're off the record. For my own tranquility."

"Oh, all right. Grow up, for God's sake. We're off the record."

Max sat up in the bed, his strong chest heaving with the effort. The mottled bruises showed against his pale skin. "I requested a leave of absence," Max explained. "With pay, since I got hurt on the job. They refused to pay me unless I stayed home. Did you know a cop's injured must stay in his house? Otherwise, the tribesmen bring you up on charges. I knew I would go mad. So I said to hell with it. I get no money but I'm free to travel and enjoy myself."

"Who is paying for your trip down here? All these expenses?"

"Simmons is paying the freight. He wants the killer caught. Just that. No side issues for him. No more government. Government doesn't serve people. They just create their own nasty little kingdoms and lock the door. Look at Al, look at Guidroz.

"They're gelded by suspicious, power-mad supervisors who want to control them. To hell with the murders. Control is more important."

"You're cynical and bitter," Diana said. "I don't like that."

"Do I care what you like? Guidroz couldn't find his suspect. The NYPD was too timid and stingy to send anyone down here to look. So I came down here, freelance for two weeks and find her. Almost got killed doing it, but I did it. So we eliminate her as a suspect. After cutting me, she's off the street and back in her madhouse where she escaped. She can't hurt anyone else."

Max stretched, the ropy muscles showing in his arms.

"Simmons wanted to learn if the New Orleans killer is the same one who killed Rusty. She probably is. That's good to know. We're tracking her now. She's leaving a trail. So I'm using Simmons' cash for what he wants. If he couldn't get me, he would have hired some private investigator out of the Yellow Pages. At least, I'm doing the work I promised to do."

"There must be some better way," Diana whipped her head from side to side.

"Oh, yeah? Tell me when you find it." He leaned forward suddenly and cupped her chin in his hands. "You are so different, Diana. You make me think about things I haven't thought about in years."

A startled smile slowly warmed her face. "What kind of things?"

"Beauty. Order. Interesting, worthwhile work where you use your head. Sexual love. It makes me want more."

"Because...?"

"Because I had half-forgotten they existed."

Diana's eyes were still vivid and angry from their argument. Max kissed her gently. She kissed him back, tasting the whiskey on his lips, then bore him back easily on the wide bed.

## CHAPTER 22.

"I've got to go to San Francisco," Max murmured from the pillow the next morning.

"It is written in the sands. Yes, sir. 'Once more unto the breach, dear friends'."

"There's been another killing, hasn't there?" Diana was wide awake by now. "I heard you on the phone last night."

"In a word, yes. We're talking off the record."

"Not that I remember." Diana had woken up feisty this morning.

Max's eyes closed. His injuries felt tender under her words. "Use me and abuse me," he said. "Treat me like a source. Have your way with my body and then wring me dry for information."

She looked over at the bedsheets and was met by his pained look.

"Coverage helps you," she said. "The more people who know about the story, the more people are out looking."

"And the more fools there are getting in the way."

"You don't have to be like those cops you tell me about, you know, 'the Budweiser tribe who play things close to the vest'. You can afford to play it looser."

As was his habit, when Max did not know what to say, he changed the subject.

"San Francisco is way overrated as a city," he said at last. "It's a foggy little garden where natives shiver their lives away inside sweaters and tweeds. But I've got to go there because there's a schoolboy killing there recently, and it fits our pattern. Whoever this killer is, she's got a taste for rich-boy blood and she's slaughtering them cross-country."

"Max, give this up," Diana said. "You tried and failed. Get back to your real job in New York. Or else you'll just turn into a hooligan, moving people around with your hands to get information. Please come back to New York with me. Or else we can't see each other anymore."

# CHAPTER 23.

The hills of San Francisco lay under Max's gaze as the Delta jet banked low over the peninsula. It was a golden morning. The Pacific Coast fog had not yet rolled in to glove the city in wet gray. The land showed great chunks of dark red earth topped with rich green grass that grew thickly in a rainy climate. The hills south of the city rose up closer and closer as the jet came down smoothly onto the runway.

Max caned his way across the airport lobby, wearing a dark blue pinstripe suit made by a Hong Kong tailor. He was alone, casting looks about him as he approached the city that many people describe as the loveliest in America.

San Francisco had grown up rapidly and glamorously, fed by the nearby gold strikes. The downtown area was sophisticated, keeping pace with its image as the Manhattan of the New West. But, like Manhattan, in the dark patches, the animals still lived and hunted.

The San Francisco killings had happened in a playground in a colorful and crowded neighborhood, on Washington Street near Kearny. The playground lay in between the Chinatown and North Beach neighborhoods. North Beach boasted strip bars and old-time beatnik coffee shops with poetry readings and jazz combos. Simmons and Max agreed that he should live as close as possible to the scene of the crime. So he paid the cheap rate of forty dollars for the two nights to the fat, bored East Indian clerk at the desk of the St. Paul hotel on Kearny Street near the killing ground.

"Look what twenty bucks a night gets you," Max murmured to himself, opening the flimsy door. "If I robbed banks, I'd live better."

The room was tiny and narrow. Max washed down a Percodan with Chivas as he unpacked sorrowfully, looking at the narrow empty bed.

He checked his notes on the killing, then when the whiskey started to cheer him, he went out into the streets half-drunk to start winning friends and influencing people so they would talk easily to him.

Max cruised merrily through the neighborhood, tipping generously and laying his name down whenever he could. He wanted everyone to know him.

☙

Lipkin was taking his first painful trip out of the hospital, in a taxi to Saint Blaise's. All the schoolboys were lined up on the street outside the brownstone school. Lipkin recognized Lily Sangster, the teacher who Simmons had brought to the hospital. He smiled for the first time in days.

"Ms. Sangster, do you remember me? Sgt. Lipkin from the Police Department." He wanted her to remember him.

Lily smiled. "Of course I do. I couldn't forget you. Should you be walking around now? I'm happy to see you, but you look very weak."

"That's what a wolf pack attack will do to you. I'm okay. Seeing you makes me feel better. What's going on here?"

"We're having a fire drill." She knew the class was listening. "Everyone behaved very well. Practically everyone. Right, Sexton?" She leaned towards a tall gawky teenager standing in line. "We almost did it perfectly, didn't we, Sexton?"

Windows went up across the street. A few Playpen residents gazed out at the well-dressed and scrubbed schoolboys.

"I'd like to speak with Mr. Pruitt, if he's free," Lipkin said.

"He's with the third-grade now. Class 3-B. They should be around," she said, walking up and down, the wind lifting her short hair.

"Where is 3-B? Martin," she called to another teacher standing nearby. "Where is 3-B? Do you have any idea?"

Nobody said anything.

"Burnt to a crisp," she said laughingly. She threw her head back. Lipkin grinned. "Sexton, go get Mr. Pruitt and bring him here."

The gawky student started at hearing his name and started walking towards East End Avenue.

"Not that way, silly," Lily said. "He's down the block. Use your head, for heaven's sake."

Blushing, the boy went back down the street.

"I probably shouldn't bother him now," Lipkin said. "Especially if there's a fire."

"Well, we never know, do we?" Lily answered. "That's why we need these drills. Right, boys?"

"That's right, Ms. Sangster," one of them chirped up.

Pruitt was not happy to see Lipkin again. That was no surprise to Lipkin. Cops either got used to being regarded as a leper, or they bailed out of the job.

"Mr. Pruitt, you've lost two boys," Lipkin said, speaking rapidly as he drew the headmaster away from his school. "I don't want you to lose any more. I'm having an anticrime team assigned to this street. Not a uniformed man like you asked me for. Uniforms scare people away. But the anticrime guys in street clothes are what we need."

Lipkin threw a look down the block.

"They'll catch anyone around your school that is stalking your boys," he said. "We may come up with the killer that way, and your school will be well protected. Don't even look for them, because you won't be able to spot them. They're very good. They're experts at blending into any street."

"I'm very grateful to you, Sergeant. I've been worried about my boys since Blake died."

"In return," Lipkin said, "I need a list of all our graduates who have ever gotten into trouble. Who have ever been institutionalized or gone into detox. And a listing of your food service, custodial and teaching staff. Their home addresses. We need to interview them away from the job here. I'll be doing it, and I'll be using kid gloves, I promise you. But I need this stuff."

"I don't like giving up gossip on alumni," Pruitt said.

"I don't like teenagers getting butchered," Lipkin shot back. "With maybe more to come. Be realistic, Mr. Pruitt. You tell me what is the greater wrong. Me hearing some juicy gossip or you having to attend another funeral? What do you think you owe your students?"

Pruitt shook his silvered head helplessly. "Six weeks ago, I would have told you to go hang," he finally said. "But this mess is changing me. I'll give you what you need, Sergeant. When the drill's over, let's sit down in my office."

Lipkin looked up and down the street, waiting patiently for the fire drill to end. Pruitt was not the only one being changed by this case.

When he was on a case, Lipkin tried never to lie to anyone except a murder suspect. He always tried to tell the truth to the witnesses. But now that was changed. He had lied to Pruitt about the anticrime team just to get his cooperation.

Lipkin knew that Quinnliven would never authorize an anticrime team. And he was going to call Lily for a dinner date as soon as possible because she was interested in him, and Lipkin liked the way she looked.

For some reason, she liked him. Lipkin was not going to question his good luck. He was breaking another rule. He had never dated anyone in a pending case. But this case was changing everyone.

※

Diana spent her first day back in New York catching up on her articles and interviews. Two editors quizzed her and criticized her for going to New Orleans, even though they had authorized the trip.

After work, she met Wendell Simmons at the Carnegie Hill Cafe on Madison Avenue and 93rd. Simmons was with a slim, athletic blonde woman, who looked to be about twenty-three years old. She sat quietly while he and Diana talked. Diana missed the woman's name but was aware of her and her expensive dress and carefree smile. She wondered what Simmons was doing with a woman like her,

"I have no problem with you knowing about Max Royster and myself and our business arrangement," Simmons said after ordering a round of martinis. "But keep it quiet, please. Or the killer might vanish. You understand that my only interest is to find the killer."

"Wendell, a good private investigator can run rings around most cops," Diana said. "Max may not be your best bet. He was not a detective but a uniformed patrolman."

"He refers to himself as just another Budweiser tribesman walking through life with the piece of lumber dragging behind him," Simmons said. "That does paint a picture, doesn't it? But he's very honest, and he's committed to solving this case."

"As an executive, I'm sure you know how to pick workers who are motivated," Diana said, leaning back as the drinks arrived. "You sure picked one in Max. But it's not healthy for him."

"Why not? He's a policeman, isn't he?" Simmons drank deeply. "I'm just barely working out my own problems now. My only consolation is Jan here. She keeps me going."

"I try to, anyway," the blonde young woman said with a faint Midwestern accent.

"I was lucky enough to meet Jan at an art show," Simmons smiled. "She is quite a painter."

"It's my therapy," the woman said. "They say it helps."

"Jan, you don't need therapy," Simmons said. "You're just joking."

Diana nodded and let her face go blank. She knew art students did not often wear expensive dresses like the one Jan was wearing. There was something wrong here. Simmons was paying for Jan's company, one way or another.

Simmons ordered another round of martinis while Diana made a list in her head. Simmons' vices might have led to Rusty's death. Tomorrow she would run a credit and background check on Simmons. He might be in tough shape financially.

Mysterious young women were expensive for older settled men.

Simmons might be losing money to Jan or some other playmate. Or he might have a cocaine habit. Diana could interview his business competition and pick up gossip.

If she cracked this murder case by herself, her reputation would sparkle throughout the city. She would get a six-figure book contract, her column and maybe later, an editor's spot, if she wished.

Diana hoped that more drinks would loosen Simmons and his friend up. But she felt the Martinis spinning her around instead. So she leaned back and listened as they discussed vacation spots for the Christmas season. Jan seemed well traveled for a young artist.

Jan's strong, shapely body showed through the dress. Jan was strong enough to strangle a teenage boy, Diana thought.

Diana criticized herself for reaching. Maybe the martinis were feeding her own violent fantasies. Liquor could do that. But she would still run a check on Simmons.

Diana put some money down for her drinks. They all swapped good-byes. She left them both there, sitting together in the night-shadowed cafe, winter gloom around them. As Diana left, Simmons shook out some small white pills into the palm of his hand.

## CHAPTER 24.

San Francisco's Chinatown was foggier than the hard-edged Chinatown in New York. Its streets sloped up and down, with pagodas arching over the heads of the tourists.

It also felt more dangerous to Max as he prowled along Washington Street near Kearny, looking for the playground where the schoolboy had been murdered.

After a half-hour, he found the playground. An alleyway ran behind it, from Clay to Washington Streets. Wooden fences ran along the alley, each fence a few feet long, each of a different style and a different type of wood. Some of the rickety buildings looked old enough to have survived the Great Earthquake of 1906.

Max referred to the photocopies in his hip pocket and then stood in the alleyway, studying the situation. Then he began to understand and picture what must have happened three weeks ago.

He closed his eyes, committing the scene to his memory and concentrating on it. Then he opened his eyes again. The alleyway started back at him. He had remembered it correctly. Now he closed his eyes and imagined that he was the murder victim.

Lipkin had taught him this trick. It was something every good homicide detective had to do, to put himself into the victim's place. Revisit the scene and walk along the victim's route. Wait where the killer waited. If the killer's path of flight was known, you should follow that path.

The homicide cop was like a stage director, setting up a dramatic scene from all possible angles. Max closed his eyes and leaned against the sagging wire fence. He knew this murder was bound to fashion some delightful nightmares for him. But it had to be done. He could try to forget about it when the hunt was over.

The playground where the boy had been murdered was just big enough for a basketball court. There were a few stone benches alongside the sagging wire fence. The mouth of the alleyway was a perfect spot for an ambush. The strangler could run in any of three directions.

The victim, David Higgins, had left his buddies in Chinatown. He told them he would take a trolley and a bus to his home in Pacific Heights, a wealthy area three miles to the northeast. Max knew all this from the newspapers. David had not planned to meet anyone else that night, his friends had said. He did not know anyone in Chinatown.

The killer had stalked him and lashed him by the neck to the wire fence. While he lay helpless and dazed, she had mangled him with her teeth and a razor blade.

"I'm betting everything that you are the same killer," Max said aloud. "Because the government is not going to help me. I have to gamble this way."

An ancient Chinese man had seen the attack from his nearby apartment window and had shouted out in broken English. Hearing him, the killer ran down the alleyway to Clay Street

The alleyway was about twenty feet wide and a hundred feet long. Max ambled down it, his scrutiny penetrating each grim crevice. He saw nothing that would help him.

"This is silly," he told himself. "You're not going to find anything here."

San Francisco Homicide would have covered this alley thoroughly with a team of forensic experts. They would have interviewed everyone living on the block to generate a composite description of the killer. The detectives would patiently grill and re-grill their only witness.

Max spent the rest of the night and the next night fighting his way through a whiskey river. He established himself on a bar on Bryant Street, across from the San Francisco Police Department Hall of Justice. He enjoyed a prime rib dinner and threw money across the bar, making friends rapidly.

The regulars relaxed around him. Some of them were homicide inspectors. On the job they were tight-lipped and suspicious but in the bar, they tended to loosen up and let things slip.

Finally, near the end of the long drunken night, Max got what he needed from a broken-down alcoholic named Dermot. Dermot somehow managed to work as a messenger at the Hall of Justice when he was not drying out at a rest farm across the Bay. Max bought him numerous whiskies and pumped him for information.

In a confidential whisper, Dermot confided that this dead boy showed bite marks all over his body. He drunkenly swore Max to secrecy on this point.

"There were other marks on the boy's body, too," he whispered hoarsely, blowing whiskey breath onto Max. "These marks could only be made by one thing. Woman's fingernails. Long ones."

He repeated this for emphasis. "Long ones!"

Max revisited the killing ground again the next night. Between his hangover and the thought of the crime that had taken place, he felt very old and depressed.

He ambled down Washington Street to a small park where old men were practicing tai-chi in the night's darkness and found a pay phone. There were some things he needed to talk up with Lipkin. He called Lipkin at home, collect.

"Al, the newspapers say she was dressed in black shiny clothes. It might have been leather." Max said, convinced it was the woman known only as Charlene.

"She's getting wilder," Lipkin answered. "She wants more attention than she did before. Wants to make people fear her. The clothes alone will do it.

"Has the Department found out anything on the Central Park killings?"

"The Department, hah! I'm doing it all on my own. On crutches. Quinnliven convinced his bosses that the killer was a transient who has already left town. So they figure there's no point in wasting manpower looking for him. I badgered the *au pair* agency about Charlene and the family she worked for. They wouldn't talk without a subpoena. Any subpoena has to be approved by Quinnliven. So that's out."

"You can't convince the brass that Charlene might be our killer?" Max asked.

"I'd have to go over Quinnliven's head to do that, which I don't want to. What I want to do is quietly check up on everyone connected with Saint Blaise's. There are a lot of strange stories coming out of that school. Some drugs. A lot of teachers have roommates. You know I don't like roommates."

"In Manhattan, everybody needs a roommate," Max said. "Especially private school teachers. They make less than cops, you know."

"I know that. Objectively. But this is a gut feeling. Most adults have roommates for the wrong reasons. They're afraid to be alone. They get their sex from the roommate. Or they dominate the roommate or want to be dominated by them. Say, that's some school that you went to. Do you know that three of the teachers have served prison time? Things in the Playpen are not what they seem.

"They never were."

"Meanwhile," Lipkin said. "You're out on sick leave. You're supposed to be confined to your home if you want to collect money from the Department. You're not supposed to be in San Francisco. They may not let you back in when you're ready."

"Back to what?"

Lipkin did not answer.

"Are you there, Al?"

"Max, you forget that I love the Department in my own complicated way," Lipkin said. "And I could never walk away from it as easily as you seem to be doing. In Blarney Stone bars, whenever someone is raging against the Department, I always say, that the Job had been good to me."

"Max, this San Francisco murder was the most vicious one yet. The other victims were strangled quick and clean. This victim was drained and quartered, strangled while he was slowly dying. The killer bit him and chewed him. Cut him in sensitive places, places where sex would have made the kid feel happy."

"You're breaking the rules, Al," Max cautioned. "You're feeding me confidential stuff for my private use. The Department would fire you if they knew."

"What you're doing is riskier," Lipkin replied. "You could wind up on the Bowery, trying to convince your fellow bums that you used to be a cop."

"Mister," a voice spoke behind Max. "How long you going to be on that phone?"

Max turned and saw two husky kids, Irish-looking with sandy hair and sunburned faces. One held a boombox radio playing rap music.

"Be off in a minute, guys," Max answered. He turned back to the phone. "Go ahead, Al."

"I won't talk with Simmons now. He's turned into a loose cannon," Lipkin said. "And you shouldn't, either. I told Simmons that this Frisco killing happened near a flophouse hotel called the St. Paul. He probably told you to set up there. Don't tell me. I don't want to know. I tried milking that teacher, Lily, for gossip. But she never answers my calls."

One of the Irish-looking boys turned up the rap music, much louder than it had been before. Max had a hard time hearing Lipkin over the noise.

"But the SFPD tells me the killer was seen near this hotel," Lipkin said. "Just after the attack. The cops screwed up. A whole week passed before they canvassed the hotel. They tried to get the guest registration cards, but the place was such a mess that it took another week. And some cards were lost. It happens, as we both know. I told the inspector in charge, some Chinaman named Tang, that he should concentrate on the hotel –"

"Gentlemen," Max said over his shoulder. "Could you please lower that music some? Thanks."

One of them laughed. The slam-bang music kept pumping out.

"Remember that this killing is fresh," Lipkin said. "New and tortuous techniques. She's getting meaner. An informant called me about a young woman training in one of these underground martial arts schools, run by teachers thrown out of legitimate karate schools. These underground schools teach people how to kill. How to strangle, how to use a knife, how to kill silently. They all flash false names, warrior names. The woman might be our killer. I'm trying to locate the school."

"I've got to go, Al. Call you later."

Max hung up the phone and turned to the two in back of him. "It's all yours now," he said.

"What are you, a wise guy?" the bigger one asked. They started circling him. They were heftier than Max had first noticed. "We're going to mess you up. Fuck you, Mister Pigeon."

"Wise guy," the other one said. "We can play our music loud as we frigging want. It's a free country."

"Home of the brave," Max agreed. He stepped forward and booted the big box radio. It bounced twelve feet onto the grass, squealing. The rap music screamed out even louder.

The closer guy jumped up as if he had been stung and rushed at Max. Max leaned back and snapkicked him once in the belly and then another time in the ribs. The other kid bounced a fist off Max's skull, stunning him for a second.

Then Max moved forward, passing him while striking him once, twice in the ribs with an elbow. The fighter yelped. Max used his foot again, kicking into the shin and then stomping down hard on the instep. The man clawed at Max's groin with his spread fingers, trying to rip something.

The first one rushed back in and tried to pin Max's arms while the other straightened up to punch. Max butted him with his head and heard the nose crack. The kid put both hands to his nose, and Max hit him with his fists, three times in the solar plexus. The kid sagged, wheezing and gasping for breath.

The other thug had gotten an arm around Max's neck and was trying to choke him. Max smelled Kahlua. Max grabbed his little finger, broke it like a pencil and then yanked. The man let go. Max jabbed him twice in the shouting mouth to set him up for a left hook punch that caught him on the side of the neck. He rolled back onto the grass, calling Max every kind of motherfucker.

"You still think you're tough?" Max wheezed, his head aching. "Want some more? I'm lucky I could take you. You're just two stupid normal drunk kids. I'm not normal anymore. If you get in my way, I'll wreck you again."

He had to get away before he fell down himself. A picture of the victim, David, flashed in his mind, tied and helplessly watching as the mad killer slowly and lovingly tortured his life away for her own pleasure.

# CHAPTER 25.

The next day was Thanksgiving.
Max felt sick with a hangover when he woke up. His beaten head throbbed where the boy had pummeled him. He lay in bed reading, drinking and dozing all day long. At sunset, he decided to go out.

Tyrannosaurus Rex was the saloon closest to his hotel, and Max decided to eat dinner there. The leggy young waitresses were dressed up like young Pilgrim maidens in black frocks and white blouses. Carnival lights were strung up and down the bar, with paper turkeys pinned to the wall.

"'Where are you tonight, Charlene?" he thought to himself, sitting at the bar. "What are you doing? Are you talking with a friend? Celebrating Thanksgiving?"

Tonight was one of those nights when the liquor hit Max hard. Sometimes it was stronger than other times. He closed his eyes for a second and imagined a strangler stalking a rich boy, walking closely behind him on the streets.

Sean, the bartender, was an expansive talker. Tonight he was holding court about Pilgrims and Plymouth Rock. The real, historical and documented reason why the Pilgrims landed at Plymouth, he said, was because they were running low on beer.

"That's right," Max agreed. "I've been to Plymouth Rock. The Pilgrims were a noble nest of tosspots and they only stopped a-sailing because they were out of suds."

Max and his wife Lisa had spent a whole week in the Plymouth settlement, exploring the woods and sampling the Pilgrim and Wampamoag Indian foods. It had been one of their best times together. But on the drive back to Brooklyn, Lisa had started to cry. Max tried to comfort here but that only made things worse. He gave up and drove grimly while she slept. Lisa had many skills and talents, but she didn't know how to let herself be happy. All her life, she had pressured herself to do more than she could. Now she was coming apart. Her family was pressing her to leave Max. They called him a bum.

And Lisa crumbled under the pressure.

"Sean, darling, can you pour some wine for a foreigner?" a newcomer's voice asked, waking Max out of his sad thoughts. "Even if I am not from your Plymouth Rock?"

"I guess we can swing that," Sean answered. "Jacky, this is Max. He's new in the neighborhood. Jacky is the reigning Grand Empress of North Beach," he explained to Max.

Max shook hands with a small woman with dark blonde hair swept up high on her head. She was darkly tanned and had sparkling hazel eyes with greenish amber flecks in them. Her eyes drew Max. Her Mexican cloth tunic revealed one tan shoulder. Her hands were small and looked capable, worker's hands, and there was a ring on every finger. Her laughing face lit up happily as she settled comfortably into the straight-backed chair.

"That is me," she said, in an accent that Max could not place. "Empress of North Beach. *Quelle vie de luxe*!"

"North Beach is in the beatnik heart of the West," Sean put in. "Hippies still survive here. Jack Kerouac, Allen Ginsberg and William Burroughs all drank in this saloon. They gave poetry readings at City Lights, just down the street. You been there yet, Max?"

"I'm waiting for someone to take me," he said.

"I'll take you," Jacky offered, sipping her Burgundy wine. "Whenever you wish. I have been in this neighborhood forever and ever." Her cat's eyes danced. "And I must know everybody here."

"Do you work here in the city?" Max asked.

"I'm still in college. At my age." She giggled, hiding her teeth behind a small thumb. Her teeth were very white and even. "I may be a student for the rest of my life," she added.

Max sent two cocktails over for the piano man and the torch singer. They both sipped and smiled their thanks before swinging into "Night and Day."

"How do you like my city?" Jacky asked. She seemed to enjoy Max's attention.

"Very individual. Has its own style. Each house is different from the next. The city is small, like a jewel of some kind. You have kept things fine and small here."

"We try to, yes. I was born in France. I came here when I was a young girl. My husband ran away from here. He talked me into moving in with him and marrying, and then he ran away, to look for fun that he could not afford when he was young. He was good at getting young girls. I remember how he got me."

"Do you like this neighborhood?"

"I like no city, really. It is better to be in the country with nature." Her French accent was clear and plain now. "That's the good way to live and work, with nature. The woods fascinate me. Natural things always make me happy. I can lie on the grass looking up at the sky. The white clouds keep moving. They never stop. They mix with the blue sky. And nobody else has time to watch them. Just me. I sit on my porch and watch the sun change all the tree colors, all the tree colors, it is beautiful. Very beautiful."

"You should see it sometime, darling," she whispered, laying a hand on his sleeve.

She had the coquette's habit of calling every man "darling," like Zsa Zsa Gabor. She gave Max her deepest attention when he talked. He was trying hard to place her way of talking. At times, she sounded like a college professor and at others, like a child learning English.

More drinks flowed. The lovely raven-haired woman singer sang:

> I can see you from miles away,
> Smiling into my dreams.

The songs, "Change Partners," "I Remember You" and "The Moon Is a Harsh Mistress" flowed out later. Max asked Jacky to dance. She fit easily into his arms. Max had left his walking cane behind for the past few days, and it felt good to be moving on his own. He felt younger and looser than before.

"I have an idea,' Max said. "It's Thanksgiving, and I've got the cash. For the time being anyway. I'd like to go back to my hotel and invite everyone there to come here for a drink. At least one drink. No one should be alone on Thanksgiving."

"That's a beautiful idea, darling."

"Noble," said Sean the bartender. "You go ahead. And if they're not already too drunk to come in, I'll match your drink with a free one from me. This is a patriotic establishment, after all."

Max found himself outside on Kearny Street surrounded by the fog, with Jacky hanging on his arm.

"'Where is your hotel, darling?" she asked.

"Just down the block. The St. Paul."

She reared back and looked at him. In the streetlights, her face appeared softer.

"But I live in the St. Paul," she said. I've been there for years. Whatever are you doing there?"

"Keeping my overhead low."

"If it was any lower, you would be living the life of a *clochard* –"

"A what?"

"Tramp. A hobo. You don't belong in the St. Paul," she said. "Not at all. There is some reason why you are here. Tell me what it is. Please. I won't tell the others." She seemed suddenly animated by the idea of a secret between them.

Max tried to blow away her suspicion. "I'm just a little low on cash, that's all."

"No, no."

A passing car's headlights walked across her face.

"There is something that you're not telling me. Your secret, yes?"

"You think that life is made up of secrets, secrets and more secrets?"

"With the men I married, yes, I do."

They were walking down Kearny Street now and passed the City Lights bookstore.

"How many husbands have you enjoyed?" he asked.

"None. But I was married five times. Bad luck follows me. My first husband, the painter, had secrets. I told him, like I tell you, to tell me the truth. And he says, no, no, it is nothing. But I know. Then one day, one of his models came in to see him, crying because he made her pregnant. I was just nineteen and stupid me, I am married to him, to 'Stinky Georgie.' That's what I call him, from that day."

"I bet that wasn't the name on the marriage license," Max observed.

"No, but that's what he is. 'Stinky Georgie.' I tell you!" she shouted, suddenly furious, stamping her small foot on the pavement. "Men! They treat me bad, and I stepping on the men! I wipe the floor with them!"

## CHAPTER 26.

Max looked at her, wondering if she could be Charlene. The thought made his hair tingle. As far as he knew, Charlene did not have a foreign accent. But maybe she did. Maybe Charlene could disguise her voice the same way that she could disguise everything else.

As quickly as Jacky's rage had come up, it subsided. She put her arm through his again and smiled sweetly.

"But not you, darling," she said. You're wonderful. I like you, whether it be Pandemonium or not Pandemonium."

"Pandemonium?"

"Pandemonium!" she sang out cheerfully. "With the demons and the devils and the Satan, they make the Pandemonium! In the Paradise Lost by the John Milting –"

"Milton."

"– that he writes about the Pandemonium. But don't worry about that. Yet."

"You can't tell if someone is Pandemonium just by looking at them," Max said.

"Yes, I can. With my experience, it's easy. Tell me, Max, are you dealing drugs? Is that why you're in my hotel?"

Max protested again that he was just low on cash. That was the only reason that he was living at the St. Paul. But Jacky shook her head sadly.

"Must be drugs. Has to be. Whenever there is something that I don't understand, I'm sure that drugs are the reason."

By knocking on different doors, they collected a mixed group of friends and hotel dwellers to bring back to Tyrannosaurus Rex. One tall, thin stooped birdlike man that everyone called 'Uncle' brought his charcoal sketchpad with him for some reason. A balding businessman with a thick moustache and a grave, professional manner said he would come along in the spirit of the thing. Kirsten and Katherine, two Swedish tourists, as fresh and open as young wildflowers, confronted Sean when they swarmed inside his place.

The final member of their party, a hefty girl, who called herself "Cathy Barr, the Folk Singer," immediately asked Sean if he had any Drambuie. There was none left in the bar. But she kept asking all night.

Max tried to mellow out, in true cool California style, as he matched Jacky drink for drink. Every now and then, pictures of the killings would flash into his mind, hanging pale heads and smashed throats. He tried to forget about them. But it was not easy.

As the night grew longer, Jacky seemed to come alive. She grew more bewitching and flirtatious. Like new lovers, they talked about everything, from the songs of Tony Bennett to the books of Lawrence Durrell and Francois Mauriac.

"Mauriac's books are old-fashioned," Max said. "No sex that you can taste. No gratuitous violence. Not like real life nowadays. For example, someone was tortured and killed in this neighborhood recently and nobody cares a damn about it. That's modern feeling for you."

"You're simplifying things," Jacky said nervously. "Who was tortured?"

"A young boy on his way home from school. It was right here. See, you didn't even know about it. And now that you know, I'll bet you don't care. That's the modern way of looking at things."

"Oh, but I did hear about this," Jacky said. "The police even came and asked everyone at the hotel if they knew anything. Debbie, did you hear about this?"

Debbie the singer was taking a break at the bar.

"About someone getting killed? Not a word," Debbie answered. "Was it a robbery?"

Max knew enough to keep his mouth shut. Let them do the talking for him.

"He was tortured," Jacky picked up what Max had said. "You don't torture someone to get his money. It might have been over drugs, some kind of revenge for a deal. It's always drugs," she said, shrugging so that her small. full breasts danced.

"Did the police come knock on your door?" Max signaled Sean for a Corona. He was growing thirsty.

"Two of them, with their little badges," Jacky replied. "But they did not listen to anything I said. I could tell they were just going through the motions."

It seemed that the San Francisco police had not canvassed this bar for witnesses. That seemed odd to Max, since it was the closest bar to the murder scene. He was starting to think that the SFPD had done a sloppy job on this case.

Jacky was talking happily with an ex-Merchant Marine sailor named Noel. Max used the opportunity to work the bar artlessly, trying to get information about the killing. It helped that everyone was getting drunk. They talked loosely.

"I been rousted by fuzz a lot, and these guys weren't too slick," a carnival worker named Dale confided, wiping beer off his Zapata moustache. "They didn't seem to care."

Max returned to Jacky again. She and Noel were talking about punk-rock clothing.

"For me, the first time I see the kids wearing crosses, I was amazed," Jacky said. "But it is not disrespectful. It is just the opposite of the yuppie philosophy. The cross shows that you are compassionate and that you care about other people and are not afraid to show it. Today we forget to show compassion. We are too busy, too suspicious, too egoist."

"So wearing a cross shows that you care," Max said, "but wearing something like black leather shows anger. Renegade behavior. Rebel without a cause. Do you know anyone who wears black leather?"

"Not now."

"Did you know someone who did?"

"There was someone at the hotel, yes,"

Max's pulse leaped once and then settled down.

"Does he still live there?"

"It was a woman. No, she's gone."

From the piano came the sounds of "Up On The Roof." Noel assembled a tenor saxophone and joined in with the two singers.

The atmosphere became increasingly festive: Sean whirled out streamers from the bar, and some of the hotel guests brought out noisemakers. The two Swedish beauties danced with each other, twirling around the saloon.

Then it was last call and Sean was dealing out drinks to the St. Paul crowd. The businessman from the hotel seemed to have discovered his wallet and was spending money freely on Cathy Barr, The Folksinger. Cathy took out her guitar, strummed a few chords and put it away when nobody paid attention. Then the whole crowd was outside on Kearny Street in a friendly rollicking band, swaying its way back to the hotel.

Since Jacky had been in the hotel the longest, she had the biggest room, and they all trooped inside.

Max looked at Jacky again, wondering if she could be Charlene. She was complicated and very angry at men. She was well traveled. Whoever Charlene was, one thing they knew about her was that she could travel freely.

Jacky had a large comfortable room, the walls painted a soft pastel. She bought out a bottle of Burgundy to share and played Laura Nyro music. Everyone talked and drank freely from paper cups.

Laura Nyro's voice must have lulled him to sleep because when Max awoke, the room was dark. The light of a candle was moving back and forth in his blurry vision. His contact lenses felt like they were glued to his eyes. He was alone with Jacky.

"I been drugged," he muttered thickly. "Shanghaied. Bound for the sex slave shops in the South China Sea."

"You were looking so peaceful, darling, so nice. I did not want to wake you." Jacky was curled up a few feet from him; so much in the shadow that he could not see her face.

"I wasn't dreaming peacefully. I had a nightmare," Max drawled. He was lying.

"On my floor?"

"I have bad dreams sometimes," he said. "But it was here in San Francisco, my dreams are in Technicolor. It wasn't fun. Thanks for waking me up."

"I didn't," Jacky said. "I was just dumping the ashtrays and picking up a bit."

For the first time he remembered, the hotel was quiet. There were no radios or TVs turned low, no muttering in the hallways. Outside on Kearny Street, everything was silent. It was one of those rare times of the quiet sounds, in the heart of a big city, where the pulse slowed down and stayed even with the breath.

"Everyone sleeps now," Max said. "The faded flower of the beatnik and hippie movements turns to bed. So many colorful life histories, fallen loves and lost dreams.

You could write a movie about people in the St. Paul. And you, Jacky, would be the star actress."

Jacky's smile glowed, softening her face.

"Other characters, too," Max said, stretching companionably. "Noel the sax player. And who was the girl in black leather that you said lived here?"

"She called herself Nancy. I didn't like her."

"Why not?"

"She frightened me. She tried to tell me about her growing up somewhere else. Her father used to beat her and then use her for sex."

"That's strange," Max said. He rested his head back on his crossed arms, closed his eyes and waited.

"What is strange, darling?" she asked after a while.

"Somehow, through your tone of voice, I picked up that you were afraid of her. You must have transferred your fear to me, in my subconscious state. That's why I had the nightmare. What did she look like?"

"She was a few inches taller than me. Most people are. And she was thin. She would have to be, to wear those tight clothes. Her hair was blonde, probably a wig because her eyebrows and eyelashes were dark. She was only here for a little while."

"How old was she?"

"I would say not more than thirty."

"Did it bother he when the police came around asking questions?

"I think that she had left by then. Maybe not. I don't remember. Why do you ask?"

"Somehow that was in my dream." He forced a smile and squeezed her hand in his. "Don't ask me why."

"She made me feel uncomfortable. But she asked me to do her favors once in a while."

"What kind of favors?" he asked, shaking himself.

"Not that favor. No, just to pick up some things for her at the store. She'd be in her room, too zonked out from drugs to move, and she'd give me a list of things to get her. So I did it. But I did not want to get close to her because she always seemed angry about something."

"Who else knew her here?"

"Nobody else. Noel said hello to her in the hall. She kept going on and on about her wretched childhood. The things she told me were quite horrible. But what could I do?"

"She knew that you have a good heart, Jacky."

"Darling."

"Did you bring food up to her?"

"No, just crap. Tylenol, mascara, eyeliner, things like that. Contact lens fluid."

"Give me another drink," Max requested. "And then I'll be rolling down the hall to my room."

"Here." She found his cup in the darkness and poured wine into it. "But you didn't see that I have here? A pillow for your head. Stay here. We'll camp out. I don't want to go into the bed. Not tonight."

"Thank you." It seemed like the safe thing to say. Sleeping here was risky. She could be Charlene. But Max needed Jacky's confidence, and this was the best way. "So we'll be bundling tonight."

"Please, what is this 'bundling'?"

"It's a Plymouth Rock Pilgrim tradition on Thanksgiving Day. An old custom brought over from England. A man and woman who were already engaged to each other would sleep fully clothed in the same bed all night long. Weren't supposed to make love to each other. That would violate the pure spirit of bundling."

"*Pour quoi?* Why?"

"So they would get to know each other before marriage and enter into it still chaste."

Jacky drew a coarse Navajo blanket over their bodies. She smelled warm and safe to Max, like a child curled up in her pajamas. He swallowed the last of his wine, feeling it bring him closer to sleep as his body relaxed. Jacky put her lips near the candle and blew it out. Now the room was all dark. She snuggled tightly against him, placed a hand on his chest and rested her head on his shoulder.

## CHAPTER 27.

After one week, Max had settled into the Chinatown-North Beach neighborhood. The bouncers and barmaids along Broadway knew him by now. So did the booksellers at the City Lights Bookstore. The Italian restaurants along Columbus Avenue fed him cannoli and cappuccino and joked with him about his tourist Italian. All the street people called him by name. It occurred to Max that he was turning into a glad-hander salesman-type who would soon start calling things 'winners'.

He sang along with Debbie and the pianist, Jay, in the Tyrannosaurus Rex about how he left his heart in San Francisco. They encouraged him to keep singing. He ate dinners with Kirsten and Katherine, the Swedish beauties, and got cheerfully drunk with everyone. He invited the desk clerks from the hotel down to the saloon for cocktails. Singh was an East Indian and Oscaro was a Filipino. Both of them liked to talk. Neither remembered any woman dressed in black leather that had lived at the St. Paul.

Covering himself discreetly, Max asked everyone about Nancy. He saw that Jacky, Noel and Debby were the most influential of his new-found friends and invited them to a

Rolling Stones concert in Golden Gate Park. He bought tickets from a scalper with more of Simmons' money.

He would kiss and hug Jacky when they met but he stayed out of her bed. Let everyone think what they wanted to. He knew he should stay as uninvolved as possible. Taking someone as a lover would close doors to him, and he needed those doors to be open. So he used the soft word and friendship to win everybody over. And despite everything, despite their own tough lives, their short-lived harsh jobs and jail stays for Driving-While-Intoxicated, the locals responded to Max. He was outgoing, friendly and generous, and he was always glad to see them. So they hung out with him and felt comfortable.

He fluttered back around Singh the room clerk, trying to find out if the cops had asked him for the hotel registration cards during their investigation. Singh remembered that the cards had been misplaced somewhere and that the Homicide Inspector, a young Asian, had threatened to shut down the hotel if nobody found them. That was the last they heard of it.

"Did you have any guests that are gone now?" Max asked.

"Lots of them. Sure."

"Which ones?"

"I don't remember, Max. Jesus, we get dozens of dingalings in here every week."

The other clerk was no better. Max realized he would have to work on word-of-mouth memory and do it fast.

ß

"Where did that woman Nancy live, Jacky?" he asked her one night when they were taking a walk down to Fisherman's Wharf to look at the tourists.

"The first floor, way in back. But why do you ask me about her again? She's not important. There's no reason for you to ask."

Max said nothing, just kept walking alongside her.

"What is the reason?" Jacky asked. "Are you still having nightmares about her? Is that what's happening?"

"This sounds silly," he said. "You never said whether she was pretty or not. Was she?"

"She looked desperate. Like she needed sleep. Men stayed away from her, even in her sexy black costumes."

"I need to know. Because in my dreams, she's the one cutting me here," Max touched his cheek. "In real life, the woman who cut me was black. But in my dream now, I see a white woman in black leather threatening me. Then I wake up. So I need to know. I want to stop these dreams."

"I understand," she said, sounding confused. "You don't show these troubles on your surface. But I'll make you feel better, darling."

"You already do. Didn't she live in the first floor, in back?"

"Why don't you try to forget her when you are awake?"

"You told me you never throw anything out. Is it possible you still have her shopping list somewhere in your room?"

Jacky laughed and said that the list might be in her room but there was no way that she could ever find it. Not in her room.

They reached the famous Fisherman's Wharf that jutted out into San Francisco Bay. Behind them, the rich green hills with their whitewashed pale houses showed in true San Francisco style. The cold waters of the Bay reflected back thousands of jeweled lights.

# CHAPTER 28.

The next morning, Max looked for the room Nancy had stayed in. He found it was empty. Nobody answered his knock.

So he told Singh he wanted to move in there. The stairs were hurting his bad leg and he wanted a room on the ground floor. Singh grumbled but told him to go ahead and stop bothering him.

The new room was better than the one Max had been staying in upstairs. It was larger and let in more sunlight. Later in the day, Max went out and bought black clothes: leather pants, T-shirts and a leather jacket.

He had heard that the old-time NYPD detectives used to break tough cases this way, by learning to live and think like the criminal. It seemed like a long shot.

"Like everything else in my life," Max thought.

He needed a plan and did not have one.

Every morning, Max walked to the public library on Kearny Street and paid to use the computers. He sent two copies of all his reports: one to Simmons and one to Lipkin. Once the reports were sent, he would brunch at the Rex, often with Noel or the Swedish girls.

Noel had been a sociology major at San Francisco State until the police staged a big drug bust. Now he was too paranoid to go back to his classes. He claimed the entire school was filled with police informants. Max knew better than to try arguing with a paranoid. A lot of the hotel guests had their own, fixed ideas. They got high regularly and that locked them into the cycle for keeps. The street had claimed them, and they would probably never cut themselves free.

Instead, Max asked Noel to examine the St. Paul guests like a true sociologist would. He suggested they start with the transients. Noel was happy to talk and show off what he had learned.

Gradually, Max worked the talk around to Nancy, the mystery woman in black leather who kept to herself. Did Noel think she was a loner, suffering from some kind of depression or inability to connect with other people?

Noel described Nancy vaguely and then rattled on some more about her. Then he went back to his favorite subject: police surveillance of free-thinkers. Max sighed and called for some whiskey to wash down the brunch. He knew that he would have to visit Jacky for more information.

Max used the Method style of acting made famous by Konstantin Stanislavsky. When he had to pretend to be drunk, he went one step beyond the Master and got drunk. He kept swapping shots of whiskey with Noel in a free-flowing talkative way until he was drunk enough to visit Jacky.

Back at the hotel, he knocked on her door with a full bottle of Chivas in his hand. The door swung open, and she took in everything at a glance. Then she touched his arm and wheedled him inside the doorway to her room.

"Oh, should you be doing this?" she asked plaintively. Her hair was unmade and hung waif-like around her face. She wore no makeup.

Max answered by going by slow and gentle degrees to her chair and then stretching out on the floor, inviting her to have a drink with him. He explained that he was trying to drown something, some bad feelings that he had. Some things that kept him awake at night and still haunted him while the sun was shining. He poured her a stiff belt and then matched it with one for himself. He talked brokenly about guilt, confusing her.

"I should have done something different, Jacky," he said, thinking about Lipkin and the gang in Central Park. "But I didn't. It keeps swinging back to me. I fucked up bad. And I can't forget about it no matter what I do or where I go. Some people can't deal with guilt. It's like they are still children and never grew up."

It was true of cops, he thought. Max was thinking like a cop. Despite his best intentions, he was starting to think like the rest of the Budweiser tribe.

He and Jacky kept drinking until he asked for some food. And then Jacky did what he hoped she would do. She left the room after he passed her some money to buy food. That would give him about twenty minutes alone in her room.

He began searching rapidly through her dresser and night table; looking for the shopping list that Nancy had given her. He pawed through all her clothing, paperback classic novels and San Francisco State textbooks.

He had talked truthfully about his guilt. It stalked him all the time. Like a true Method actor, he had managed to get himself drunk and sad in order to play this scene well.

His fingers flew through the desk drawers, through canceled checks and photos. Transients like Jacky usually did not have many personal papers. It was too much trouble to pack the papers up every time they moved to a new place. So, like musicians or gypsies, they traveled light.

Suddenly he found it and was holding it in his shaky fingers. The list was a torn scrap of graph paper with penciled writing on it in script. It read

        Tylenol
        Mascara
        Robitussin cough syrup with codeine
        Scotch tape
        Eye liner
        Crest toothpaste
        Soft-lens contact lens fluid

    This is it, he told himself excitedly, the key to the kingdom. It was his first bit of trace evidence to the killer.

# CHAPTER 29.

He heard a floorboard creak. Max flung himself around in a fighting crouch, fists suddenly up and hardened to throw punches. Then he realized that the noise came from the hallway. Jacky was coming back. He shoved the dresser drawer shut with the flat of one hand. The hallway door started to open. He sprawled himself silently back onto the floor, banging both his knees on the planks. The pain choked him as his legs, still bruised from the beating, twisted against the floor. He bit down on the inside of his cheek to keep from shouting with the pain. His head went down fast. Jacky would think he had been sleeping.

"Are you all right, darling?" she asked, opening the door and coming through it. "Noel said he would get the food. I told him I was worried to leave you alone. So he'll bring the food. He is a nice man, darling. Compassionate."

Max still had his fists balled up as he lay on the floor. He could feel the scrap of paper in his fist. Chattering to distract Jacky, he slipped the note into his jeans hip pocket. Safe. He had made it. He finally had the note. He poured himself a stiff straight shot to celebrate. The whiskey rocked him.

"Ah, no," he heard Jacky saying. "You drink too much. I never knew a man who was worth a damn who didn't drink too much."

He stayed alone on her floor all night, using the whiskey to blunt himself into sleep. He was afraid to touch Jacky or talk too much with her because he might somehow lose the note or say the wrong thing and give himself away. It was getting harder and harder to play his character role in the hotel.

# CHAPTER 30.

The next day he wrote his two reports, photocopied the shopping list and mailed the original to Lipkin. The DA's office could not issue a subpoena for a sample of Charlene's handwriting from the *au pair* agency in New York. This shopping list might prove valuable, to prove that Nancy was also their New York killer. It could make their entire case.

These were the thoughts he was thinking as he came back into the hotel whistling softly and met Diana Calia coming down the narrow staircase. Her chiseled face suddenly lit up when she saw him.

"What are you doing here?" he snapped. His hand went onto her arm automatically and started to pull her down the stairs. "Don't say a goddamn word. Nothing. You got that?"

`That's nice talk, Max," she tried to pull her arm free. "Three thousand miles –"

"Can it. You weren't invited."

He was trying to get away from the registration desk before anyone noticed them together. But it was too late. The glass door at the top of the stairway opened and then closed. Someone had seen them. Max could not see who it was.

He hustled Diana down onto Kearny and walked her into the nearest alleyway where nobody would see them together. Many of the locals knew him by sight now. He was a local celebrity along this street, because of his flame-colored hair and his freewheeling, raucous partying.

"You look even younger and more vulnerable than you did when I met you," he said whistling up a cruising cab. "You look wonderful to me, Diana."

She was pleased, even though her body reacted angrily against being manhandled. "Now, that's nice talk."

She was relieved when he got into the cab with her.

"Where are you staying?"

"Can't I stay with you? I didn't get a hotel yet."

"My friend, take us to the Hyatt on Union Square," Max told the driver. He was a bored-looking fat Filipino wearing his gray hair in a long pigtail and balancing wire-rimmed glasses on his nose. He looked like an Asian Ben Franklin.

"You have gone screaming nuts here," Diana said. "I thought you would. All by yourself in a flophouse. What makes you think I can afford the Hyatt?"

"You can't. But Simmons can."

The driver swung into the four-cornered park that San Franciscans called Union Square. Water jetted up from the fountains, gushing white. Tourists walked by, window-shopping at the jewelry stores.

The driver stopped at the wide stone entrance, ahead of a long line of other taxis. Max paid him, left a good tip and helped Diana out onto the sidewalk. The driver parked the cab and got out to talk with other drivers. His pigtail waved in the breeze. When he turned his back, Max stared. Taped with masking tape across his tweed jacket's back, the words LOVE IS THE ONLY ANSWER announced his feelings to the world.

Diana wrapped herself up in the feel and warmth of Max, trusting to him with her eyes closed. They woke up sometime in the afternoon, rolled over in their bed and went back to sleep.

"I had to move you away from my hotel," Max explained, toying absently with her smooth cheek as she laid her head on his chest. "I'm not supposed to have any question mark about me. I'm just Max to them. A modern, existential man, living briefly for today. My character can't stand to be alone so I continuously carouse and whoop it up with the neighborhood worthies. A beautiful woman from my past would start them wondering. And I can't afford that. It would cost me weeks of work."

"Simmons told me where you were living," Diana said. "He thinks I'm good for you."

"You feel good to me. That's for sure."

"But while you're theorizing about what your character should be doing, like this is an experimental play, are you getting any closer to Charlene? Or are you just living the way you like? On Simmon's money. Turning this crusade into some kind of a cop junket? What have you found out?"

Max knew he couldn't tell her about Nancy or anything else. She might print it. That could destroy all of his careful work.

"I've done okay," he said. "They accept me. Because of my cash, they call me King. 'King Max of the Saint Paul'."

"I'll bet they do."

"That's a powerful idea. I've always rather fancied that I should be a king of some kind. You can't beat the income bracket, for one thing. And since you run the joint, you can make your own tax laws. It's a lot like the fat cats in Washington do right now."

"And I'll bet you can get all the ladies in the kingdom, too," she said. "*Droit de seigneur?*"

"Most ladies see themselves as some kind of queen. And unless you can convince them that you are some king-type guy, they will not give you a shot of leg."

"You can't hurt me, Max. I know when you are joking." She sounded hurt. "You think this killer is someone with a regular job and life in New York. That's impossible. How could she get all this time to travel?"

"People keep beating me over the head with that," he said. "You and Quinnliven. She could be a traveling professional something. Let's go back off the record. I know it's silly but it's necessary."

He waited to see her nod.

"The boy here was killed on Saturday. Hotel people remember that my suspect left town the next day. That would explain why the SFPD never paid her any attention or interviewed her. I've gotten closer. I've talked to people who knew her and what she looked like. How very strange she was."

"Give me something I can print."

"I can't."

"Are you sure she really exists?"

"You traveled a pretty long way just to pick a fight with me," he said. Diana had him backing up now, feeling defensive.

"I came here because I needed to. To see you. To see what's real and what isn't. What is valuable and what is not?"

"There's more than that," Max said. "Your paper did not send you. Interest in the case has died down. The citizens are calm. But you know I'm getting close out here. You told me once that you were tight with a buck. But you flew out here on your own nickel. Why?"

"You might become a detective yet."

He could sense her smile in the darkness. She answered him with a question. "Do you have any idea if our relationship will work out or not? I have to know now. Because there is somebody in New York who is serious about me."

"Somebody in San Francisco, too."

"You see? You don't show it to me. I have to ask. Is that the way it's supposed to be? I don't think so."

She was so lightly built that she could lie easily on his chest. He breathed happily with her sweet weight on him.

"He wants to marry me, Max. What do you want to do with me?"

He felt stung in the darkness. He was glad she couldn't see his face. "I should be working on this case," he whispered. "Before Lipkin called me to help out, I was quietly despairing of ever being happy in the Department. The sergeants were going to keep me miserable. Strange as it sounds, Rusty Simmons dying reminded me that I have some use. Then you woke me up further and showed me that I could still enjoy things."

"This is a crusade for you," she said. "Another adventure. Like shipping out to Hong Kong. Is that why Lisa left you? Because you refused to grow up and stop gallivanting around like some kid? You weren't willing to make the required changes and grow together with her."

She was accusing him.

"It hurts me to hear Lisa's name. Please don't say it."

"Lisa, Lisa, Lisa. Now that you have all this renewed purpose in policing, what are you going to do with it? Stay here and degenerate? Because that's just what you're doing."

"What do you want me to do? Give this up and go back with you to New York?" Max asked. "Tell Simmons I ran out of juice? So the two of us could successfully buffet this marriage proposal that you're wrestling with now?"

It was time to get out of this bed.

"I won't do that, Diana. I'm sorry that this fella is so tempting and agreeable to you. But I won't shut this case down to keep you with me."

She breathed out and twisted off of him. The voice that she used was thinner and colder than he had ever heard before. "Then it seems like we're wasting each other's time, doesn't it?"

The words hung in the quiet air of the hotel suite. He waited for the hurt to leave him and then he waited some more.

But the hurt stayed with him.

## CHAPTER 31.

When Max woke up the next morning alone in his bed, he was hungover and slow moving. His fight with Diana had hurt him badly. He was glad to get outside in the sunlight and take breakfast with Jacky at the Tyrannosaurus Rex patio.

"Oh, there is something I should show you," she said suddenly. "Noel took my picture in the hotel. In the background, there is that psycho girl, Nancy, who gives you nightmares. She got in the picture by accident. If you saw her face, maybe your bad dreams might stop. Do you want to see it?"

"Very much. Thank you, Jacky." Max wanted that snapshot. "You can show it to me after brunch."

Max paid for the meal and they left together. He was humming his song absent-mindedly, the song that reminded of him of his wife. Jacky's body brushed against his.

"You're always humming that Holst," Jacky murmured. "Every day."

"What do you mean 'that Holst'?" Max asked. "What are you talking about?"

"Don't you know that music? You whistle it all the time. It's from Gustav Holst's symphony, *The Planets*.

The part you hum is called 'Jupiter, the Bringer of Jollity'. That part is the warmest, sweetest, friendliest music in the entire symphony." Jacky beamed. "That part was so pretty that when the London Symphony Orchestra first played it, the cleaning women heard it, put down their mops and danced with each other in the halls."

"And I've been humming it for years, not knowing what it was," Max said. "It must have stayed in my mind from when I was married."

"Was your wife a musician?"

"I still don't know what she was."

They turned back towards the hotel, dodging a running stream of Chinese children, hooting and skylarking.

"You clear up all my mysteries for me, Jacky."

"Yes, darling. The crazy Nancy and your music."

They entered the hotel. Max felt more and more tense around the hotel. He felt like his cover was blown. Others avoided him. Diana's visit had shaken him up badly.

Noel stood in the long narrow stairway that led into the lobby from the streets. He was talking with a stranger in a black leather jacket, heavy spurred sideburns and silver bikers' jewelry. Noel did not look up as Max and Jacky passed him. That was very bad, Max told himself, a bad sign. As soon as Max got that snapshot, he was leaving this hotel.

They passed by the front desk. Singh was talking with a tourist, a bulky big man in a dusty black raincoat with a short grey beard. His blue eyes were roaming wildly over the lobby. Max took him for a drug user, someone wild who was on his way up or down, depending on the supply.

"Jacky, let's go back and eat," Max said. He wanted to get outside safely with her. "I just got hungry again."

"You want to go now?" she asked. "I don't –"

"You talk that way to me?" the tourist suddenly roared at Singh. "You fucking monkey! I'll blow your head off!"

His hand reached under the raincoat. Max took one long step back. Singh was trying to get under the desk but he was moving too slowly.

"No! No!" he whimpered. "Don't do it, sir!"

"Police officer!" Max bellowed automatically. "Police! Don't move!"

His foot slammed into the tourist's belly just as the blue-steel gun cleared the belt. His kick slammed the tourist through the double doors and down the stairway where Noel and the stranger were talking.

The tourist smashed against steel-edged steps. He went down twenty feet to the street. His gun clattered and bounced next to him.

Max went to the doors. He looked down in time to see the tourist hit the last step. Noel scooped up the gun. The tourist was harmless now, bloodied and moaning. Max started to relax.

"Who's the cop?" Noel shouted, raising the gun toward Max. "You? You said 'police'! I heard you, man."

"Naw, naw, that's bullshit, Noel," Max said. "I had to say something to stop him."

"Bullshit, man!" Noel shouted, his old paranoia raging again. "I heard you! You're a fucking cop!"

"A cop? He's a cop?" Noel's buddy in the black leather jacket started up the stairs towards Max.

Singh and some others crowded out onto the landing, watching the battered tourist. "You got me dealing in front of a cop!"

"Max is a cop!" one of the Swedish girls shouted out behind him. "King Max!"

Noel triggered a shot. Max scrambled back inside the double doors. The crowd broke and ran. Max ran for his room. He figured he could get out the window into the garden and away somehow. Two more shots sounded. Singh sagged to the floor, crying out in some foreign tongue. Jacky was frozen to where she stood. The Swedish girl, Kirsten, stopped near the desk, swinging her big shoulder bag around like a shield. Her blue eyes caught Max's.

"Kirsten! Get down! Hit the floor!"

"Max!" she said. "Fucking Max!"

Noel appeared at the head of the stairs and stepped over Singh.

"You, Noel!"

Another gun showed in Kirsten's hand, coming free from the shoulder bag. It flared and jumped.

Max went down on the plank floor and rolled. More shots popped in the lobby. Max covered his head and kept rolling until he hit a wall. Kirsten was shrieking now, out of control.

Noel fired again. Jacky screamed. Max flattened himself out. Noel went backwards through the same doors and pinwheeled down the stairs again until he stopped next to the other gunman.

Max saw Kirsten lying like wet laundry, her child's blonde face stiff, and the china blue eyes blank. Max automatically wrenched the gun away from her still hand.

Blood covered her white peasant blouse, coming out between her fine young breasts. She wore no bra. Max touched her neck artery. It was hopeless. A slug had hit her lung. He watched the bright red artery blood empty her life onto the lobby's plank floor.

The gun was a cheap foreign-made .38 revolver, he noticed. Max scrambled to his feet and moved swiftly and crabwise, not making a target as he moved up to check on Singh. The room clerk was still alive, moaning and weeping like a whipped puppy.

"Jacky, call the cops," Max said. "Ambulance. Use the desk phone."

"I can't."

"Do it now."

"They'll get me! I can't, Max."

He ignored her and slammed the bullet-shattered doors open, training the gun two-handed down the stairway at Noel's body. He breathed in deeply, making sure that Noel had stopped moving.

This was the dangerous part, he told himself. This is when cops get killed. When it looks like it's over.

He sighted on Noel's tie-dyed T-shirt and again flattened himself against the wall so he would not make a target.

The door slammed against his elbow. Jacky was out on the landing, trying to run away. He grabbed her with his free hand and yanked her back, away from Noel.

"Where do you think you're going?"

"Max, please let me go! Please!"

"Fuck that. Get on the wall. Get on the fucking wall!" He positioned her against the wall and frisked her quickly. "You move and I'll hurt you. I'm getting tired of guns coming out of nowhere."

"Max, no!" Her blonde curls shook as she wagged her head.

"Leave me alone with these stiffs? No way, pal. Go use that phone."

One of the doors opened upstairs. Max wheeled around and saw Katherine walk down the stairs. She saw Kirsten lying in blood.

"No! No! NOOOO!" she threw back her head and screamed.

Max heard car doors slamming and police radios gurgling downstairs. The first cops were already coming up carefully on Noel and the other gunman, their service guns out and gripped two-handed like Max had done. Max laid the Saturday Night Special on the desk and gripped Jacky's belt with both hands. The shakes were finally getting to him. She was weeping now, her mouth twisted and ugly as she cursed Max.

"You up there! Police! Come out with your hands up!"

"Max," she moaned. "I want to die."

"That can be done easy right now. Sit down here and don't move. I'll go outside. I know the magic words."

"Police! Come out!"

"I'm coming down!" Max shouted back. "I'm a New York cop! You've got two hit up here and two female civilians. I'm opening the door now."

"Do it careful!"

Max slowly edged the door open with his elbow, making sure that his hands were high and empty. A dozen blue uniforms were bunched up in the narrow hallway, handguns trained on him. He saw a pump shotgun.

"I'm a cop," he repeated. "ID in my wallet. What do you want me to do?"

"Just walk down," the shotgunner said. "Real slow."

He made it down to the ground level. Noel was out by now, the gun lying next to him. The nearest cop gripped Max's hands and speed-cuffed him. The others bounded past him up the stairs.

"I want to talk to Tang," Max said. "Inspector, Homicide. "He'll know what this is about. Give him a call, will you?"

## CHAPTER 32.

Singh died in the ambulance on the way to the hospital. Max, Jacky, Katherine and some others were brought down handcuffed to the Hall of Justice and interrogated by different cops in different rooms.

"Okay, Mister," said a bald-headed Inspector with a heavy walrus moustache. "I hear you're a cop. Let's see something."

Max opened his wallet and took out a folded photocopy of his police identification card. His hair was much shorter in the official photo.

"Looks okay. But where's the original?" the Inspector asked.

"Back in New York. I'm on leave of absence. We're not allowed to carry the shield or ID card during that time. The Department's still holding them."

"I'm sure that photocopying them is a violation of some kind."

"So am I. Everything else is."

"I'll buy the I.D. for now. Okay, you're a cop. Tell me what happened."

"I'm a New York cop," he repeated. "On leave because my partner and I got hurt on a murder case. The killer came to San Francisco and lived in the hotel. That's all I can give you now. I want to talk to a Legal Aid lawyer before I say anything more."

"You're fucking with me? You want Legal Aid?"

"Yes, officer. Sorry. But I have to. You know why. And I want some medical attention, too. I'm feeling the stress from all that shooting. After I get some help, I'll give you whatever you want."

The Homicide Inspectors put Max inside a holding pen deep inside the Hall of Justice. The pen was filled with the polyglot world of carefree rowdy San Francisco. Samoans, Filipinos, Chinese, Mexicans, blacks and some lonely-looking white guys like Max were crammed together near a few steel benches, trying to tell themselves that it wasn't too bad. Max felt like he could start crying.

Pictures of Kirsten lying in her own blood, Katherine's screams and Jacky's hysteria nailed their spiked way into his mind. He could not shake it loose, any of it. He stretched out on the stone floor in his blue jeans and plaid shirt and tried to sleep but it was impossible.

The talk surged and ebbed around him. Some of the prisoners were clearly insane, lying in their own filthy rags and hooting whenever anyone came near them. One made monkey sounds and scratched his genitals with filthy, broken-nailed fingers.

After an endless night, two deputies brought him out of the cell and walked him upstairs to a small gray room marked "Attorneys." One did a quick frisk on Max and handcuffed him to the metal chair. Another deputy came in, holding Jacky by the elbows. She was rear-cuffed and looked awful. Tears had streaked down her face.

"Why are they holding you here, Jacky? You didn't do anything." Max said, wanting to comfort her. "This is just a formality. I'll get us both out of here."

"Darling," she whispered. "Darling, no. You can't do that. That's why I tried to run away. My first husband,

'Stinky Georgie', you remember, he had them put me in a mental hospital after I hit him with a hammer. The judge was angry with me. The hospital was terrible. If I stay there, I go crazy for real. So I escape the Pandemonium. I run away. Live quietly and very nice. But now they catch me, darling. Because of you."

"Come on," one of the deputies said. "Stand up."

She avoided his hand.

"You, darling!" she shrieked at Max.

Orderlies in white uniforms came inside the room. Max heard Velcro rasp.

They fitted restraints over Jacky's small body. Max tried to move but the handcuffs stopped him. A deputy shoved him down. Jacky was trying to bite. One of the orderlies punched her. Another grabbed her around the waist, grinning lewdly.

"She's a handful," the orderly said.

"Can't you wait? You'll have plenty of time for that later."

The other orderly smirked. "So will I."

"Darling! Darling! I never going to get out now!"

The orderlies dragged her kicking and screaming out of sight. Max shook his head when the deputy who had shoved him down offered a Camel from his pack. Jacky's shouts faded away in the corridor.

A chunky Asian man with a round Buddha's face appeared in the doorway.

"You're Royster, right? I'm Tang, Inspector out of Homicide. They say you want to talk to me about the David Higgins killing. What have you got to trade?"

"If you get me out of here, I'll waive my right to a lawyer and give you someone for the killing. Let me leave California. I've done no crimes here. I just don't want to spend six months in jail as a material witness to the murders in the hotel."

He waited. Tang kept scanning him. Then he finally nodded.

Max told him all about the New York and New Orleans murders and about Nancy in the St. Paul Hotel. Being afraid made Max eloquent. He understood how cops and prosecutors thought. This was his only way to get out of this mess. He knew he was very close to a jail term now.

"Let me call the Deputy District Attorney and sound him out," Tang said. "Noel has a fractured skull from his fall down the staircase, and he's not expected to live. Plus, he has three slugs in him from the Swedish girl's gun."

"It was drugs, wasn't it?"

"Naturally. The two Swedish girls had a few ounces of coke hidden in their rooms. They were dealing to North Beach street peddlers so they could prolong their vacation here. And they dealt to Noel. Noel was dealing with another guy in the staircase when he made you as a cop. Suddenly, everyone had a gun. And they all suspected each of informing to you, the cop. Paranoia comes with the drug business. There was not time for a chat."

Tang shook his cherub's head, circled by blue cigarette smoke.

"Kirsten was only seventeen-years old," he said. "The other one said that you turned her down once. She doesn't like you for that."

Tang and the deputies left him there handcuffed to the chair. Hours passed. Max could not sleep. He tried to think about "Jupiter, the Bringer of Jollity" and hummed it.

Finally, the sky outside brightened. Birds sang. Sunlight came in. Then Tang showed up, wearing a different suit, looking rested and sure of himself. Max felt his own fear freeze him.

"No deal, Royster. The DA says you stay here. Let's go."

"Where are we going? You left me here so long I'm starting to like it," Max bluffed.

"I'm throwing you back into the holding pen. In a couple of days, you'll come before a judge, and I'll get you remanded as an uncooperative material witness. Case should come to trial in about eight months against Katherine."

Max shrugged and let Tang lead him handcuffed down the hall. He could not let Tang see his fear. He had to keep bluffing.

"You can still talk to me and save yourself eight months in the joint," Tang said. "Otherwise, you're inside."

"Only if I can leave. So jail me. I've always wanted to lose this belly."

"You're stepping on your own dick."

"You do paint a picture."

They kept walking toward the pen. Then Tang cursed in Cantonese and led Max back to the attorney's room.

"Why, officer? Tell me why," Max said in Cantonese. "*Dimguy ging-shaw? Wang oh jee?*"

"You were in Hong Kong long enough to learn some words, huh? You're a freak, pal. Okay, we'll do it your way. The Deputy DA gave his okay. Let's start."

Max ordered two roast beef sandwiches on sourdough bread with Dijon mustard and some Anchor Steam beer. Then he started talking. Tang ran a tape recorder.

Max talked about the killings in New York, New Orleans and San Francisco. He touched on everything except Wendell Simmons and Diana.

Tang questioned him expertly, using the same offhand style as Lipkin. That cheered Max a bit. It was like talking to Lipkin. They ate together while the tape was transcribed.

"Forget about your clothes at the hotel," Tang said. "Forget about San Francisco. I'm having a deputy put you on the first plane out of here. Don't do any comparison shopping at the airport. You fucked around in this case and some people are dead because of you. I don't know how you'll live with that, but you won't do it here. Now get out of my town."

## CHAPTER 33.

Max flew back to New York in the black clothes that had become his trademark look in Chinatown. He always carried all his cash with him since it was safer there than in his hotel room. When he touched down in New York, there was a light dusting of snow on the ground.

He took a taxi to his apartment in the Playpen, telling himself that it would be his last luxury for a while. Exhaustion shook him. He coughed and felt like vomiting. The taxi took forever to get him home. When he got to his apartment and saw the forgotten heaps of clothing and food in the icebox, he sank onto his futon and fell asleep.

ø

On the other side of Central Park, Diana stirred in her sleep and moved her hands across the mattress. The curly-haired young man sleeping nude alongside her said something that she was too drowsy to hear. She subsided sleepily again. Layering herself in more and more sleep, feeling good that she could keep sleeping. Sleep, sleep, sleep, she told herself luxuriously, yawning with her chiseled, catlike face.

The table in the dining room still held the china dinner plates set for fourteen guests. Ashtrays over-flowed with cigar stubs. The prime rib of beef lay cold on the center plate. Empty champagne bottles, laid on for an engagement dinner, lay around the room.

☙

The next day Max met Lipkin for lunch at Giambone's restaurant in Little Italy. Lipkin was surprised at how Max had changed. His boyish face had aged, the skin stretched tighter over the bones. His skin was paler than usual and pulpy. He did not look like an outdoorsman any more. He looked like a drinker who spent time worrying indoors. His hands moved quickly and jerkily, with a feverish kind of speed.

Max leaned his growing belly back in the chair and told Lipkin everything that had happened. Tony Giambone came from behind the bar and brought over a carafe of the Portuguese white wine that he kept in stock for his friend, Lipkin. Lipkin nodded and sipped the wine and made notes in his ringed notebook. Max sucked the wine down like his belly was on fire.

A bulky man with silver-colored hair and awkward workers' hands came through the Giambone tables. He nodded deferentially to the District Attorney and other bosses who were lunching there and came to Lipkin's table.

"Where do they get these ploughmen?" Max mumbled. "Right off the gangplank from County Cork and onto the Job."

"Relax, Max." Lipkin got up to shake hands warmly with the ploughman, who opened a shy mouth full of corn-colored teeth. "Meet Captain Andy Meara. Cap, this is PO Max Royster."

"How you doing?" the Captain gripped mitts and pulled out a chair. Then he ordered a John Jameson's with a splash and told Lipkin that things were very bad now, and he didn't know if he could help.

"Help what?" Max asked crudely.

"Help getting you back on the Job," Meara said shortly, his voice rising automatically "Sorry, but you don't know the humps they got working over there now."

"Oh, yes, I do."

"Max, how did you get on the Job at the age of forty-two?" Meara asked. "I never heard of a rookie that old. The cut-off is thirty-five."

"When I passed all the tests, the Department delayed my appointment," Max smiled. "So I went a-traveling. The Job never contacted me again. Never tried to. By the time I was forty-two, I realized that I had to cover up my wild life with something that could pass for some kind of career. So I went into court and acted as my own attorney, suing the city to get on the Job. Superb performance. I claimed that the city was negligent in not following up. But I didn't really want the Job."

"You wanted the money," Lipkin said.

"Cash," Max stressed it. "Greenbacks. Pictures of the dead Presidents. Boy, did I want that money! But I gave too good a show, weeping and raging about how I wanted to protect the weak and smite the wicked. The judge paid close attention to my vocabulary and different poses. He bought the whole act. If wanted the Job that badly, I could have it. No cash award. But he signed the papers allowing me to get the job that I had always wanted."

Meara looked at both Max and Lipkin to see if he was being kidded.

"You can't get on the Job that way," he said.

"But he did," Lipkin said. "And just so you don't think Max is a waste, he got four Meritorious Police Duty awards in the first year. And he finished first in his class academically. He was my best student there. So he's worth saving."

"That's the craziest story I ever heard, and I've been on the Job twenty-seven years," Meara said. "Every crazy story about getting on. But you beat them all."

"Can he get back on?"

Meara shook his big head sorrowfully. "Not yet. They want him to see the Department surgeon first. Then the Department shrinks. It will take a while. It's his own fault. If he had stayed on Injured-On-Duty status after you guys were both hurt, he would be in the clear. Now they want to make him go the whole nine yards. And that lawyer Decker is suing the city because of Max hurting his client on an arrest. Two million bucks worth."

"If I were on Injured-On-Duty status, I would have had to stay in my apartment," Max said.

"Andy, she's a whacked-out karate nut from New York who travels. Max had to travel to track her."

Meara spread his huge hands. "Hey, rules are rules. The message from San Francisco didn't help things, either. He must have pissed off somebody a while back."

"Almost everybody," Max said. "Everybody in the Job. They would all sing at my wake."

"There's another thing about Max you should know," Lipkin said. "He scored. He hit the jackpot, Andy. Max doesn't know this yet. But I finally got a sample of Charlene's handwriting from the New York *au pair* agency. I put it against a shopping list written by the San Francisco suspect. They match."

Lipkin breathed out harshly, glowing with a fierce hunter's pride.

"They were written by the same person. Across three thousand miles and two hundred and eighty-six million people, Max tracked the real killer with no gun, no shield and no authority. He's worth saving."

"You might have told me before," Max said. "So the same woman did kill all these boys."

Meara scanned him again. "If Al says it, I buy it. You really did it, didn't you, Royster? This calls for a drink."

When Meara had left, Lipkin looked sorrowfully at Max, wagging his head.

"The game isn't over yet, Max," he said. "I'm going to keep pushing until I get you back on the Job. There's no way they can keep you off."

"Not legally, no. But since when did that ever bother them? The bosses do what they want. They always have. You get blown up or shot and then you have to fight in court for a pittance of money. It's a low, vicious, poisonous way to live up there in the backstabbing upper reaches of the Department."

"But you didn't do any crimes."

"I didn't kowtow to them, didn't show them Irish schoolboy respect. Which, to them, is the worst crime of all."

Max left Giambone's feeling played-out. The case was over. He stopped by his bank to learn that he had less than three hundred dollars to his name. He automatically looked at the robbery cameras in the bank's corners and the fat, sleepy Wells Fargo guard. His face looked like very pale candle wax badly molded by an idiot child. This was a bank that he could easily rob in good conscience. There was no real security.

Then he could fly to Cannes afterward and soothe whatever conscience troubles he had with lobster and cold champagne.

Max wanted to leave New York now. The Department was not going to rehire him. There were only a few reasons for him to stay around.

℘

Diana picked up her telephone on the first ring and said that she was glad that he was back in New York.

"I get the feeling I don't belong here," Max said from the payphone. "That I came back too soon."

"As far as I'm concerned, you came back too late," she said. Something cold fingered Max in the heart.

"You should have stayed out there," Diana went on crisply. He knew this voice now. It was something that she used on strangers. "You were so enthusiastic about what you were learning there. You drove me away. Snubbed me. Now you're back. Did you catch Charlene?"

"You would have heard if I had," he said. Suddenly, he felt very tired.

"So you came back empty. Maybe you finally ran out of money. Or lost your nerve. Why don't you tell me what happened?"

Max's words were getting hard for him to say. "Something happened. I didn't want to tell you over the phone."

"Well, whenever you want to talk about it on the phone, you can give me a call. But right now, we're wasting each other's time. Goodbye, Max."

☙

Max walked uptown through the ancient red-brick buildings of Little Italy. He watched old grandmothers dressed in black shuttle across the narrow streets, loaves of bread smelling warm and fresh from the bakeries. Older men sat inside private clubs over tiny espresso cups, gnarled hands moving as they talked.

The old men's lonely worn faces reminded Max of Simmons. He still owed Simmons a final report, to wrap things up.

Max shook himself from the chill and started dialing on a payphone.

## CHAPTER 34.

When Simmons arrived at the Carnegie Hill Cafe, he found Max sprawled out on one of the sidewalk chairs, looking over the menu. Max looked worried, as if he were deciding what he could afford now.

"Let me do this right off," Max said, pushing an envelope across the marble table. "This is your expense money back, with an accounting of everything I spent. It's all there. The arithmetic may be a little woozy at times but I was often drunk when I wrote it. That's the way I had to operate, as you know."

"The room was cheap, anyway," Simmons smiled, motioning for a menu.

"At the St. Paul? Very cheap. But it was worth your life to go into the halls."

They ordered their food. Max told Simmons everything that had happened.

"The trail is broken then," Simmons said. "I could get Nancy's snapshots from Jacky somehow. That picture is the most valuable thing I see now. Can you do it for me?"

"I can't go back to San Francisco."

"You learned a lot out there. You did much better than I would have thought possible. You're a good detective. The Department will recognize that and reward you for it eventually."

"They're taking their time about it today," Max said wryly.

"You could talk to Jacky wherever they have put her. She wouldn't withhold from you, would she?"

"If I show up anywhere in California in the next five years, I risk getting arrested for accessory before the fact in several killings. Those cases with the hotel killings will be in court. The DA only let me leave the city because he needed the information I had to prosecute what would otherwise have been a difficult and mysterious drug-related shootout. The court might still issue a bench warrant for me. They would want me to testify, under pain of a contempt charge, about what happened. I don't want to make it easy for them by being available."

Simmons leaned back in his chair as his whisky arrived.

"Wouldn't they extradite you from New York anyway?"

"No. Too expensive. Too many bosses would have to approve it. It's tough to extradite a witness interstate. My New York lawyer could block it easily. And I don't plan on being available to anyone here, either."

"Well, if that's how you feel, I understand. I'll use a private agency. I don't see anything further for you to do in this case. Do you have any idea where Charlene might be now?"

Max shook his head, breathing out heavily. He felt like he was a thousand bitter and long years old.

"Do you have any idea where we might find her?"

Max knew he could stretch out this junket in the good life by stringing Simmons along now. He could talk his way into taking another trip, somewhere new, and let Simmons support him. But that would not be fair.

So he shook his head, not trusting his mouth to say the right thing.

"Well, that settles things. You'll be going back on the Police Department and I'll be taking a holiday trip pretty soon."

"The Department doesn't seem to know that I'll be coming back. Where are you going for vacation?"

"Wherever my friend decides," Simmons said. "Someplace warm. Away from all this." He sighed. "I hope somebody stops this killer. But I can't do any more. Rusty dead. I still can't credit it. My boy is dead. His sisters will be in therapy for the rest of their lives. But life goes on."

In the dark cynical part of Max's mind, he saw that Simmons had already accepted his loss and was willing to trade Rusty's memories for orgies with young women. Lipkin had told Max that Simmons was using up the hookers provided by the rougher escort services. As if he thought keeping young women in his bed would keep him young.

Simmons might have been quiet and restrained with women before Rusty died. Or he might have been sampling these same dangerous women and doing expensive drugs. He might even have an idea who killed Rusty.

Lipkin had taught Max never to trust anyone in a case. Lipkin also said that Simmons' choice of playmates looked like rough leather girls who were capable of anything.

Max grunted to himself. This case was driving him nuts if he suspected Simmons.

"If you think I'm a good detective, listen to me," Max said. "Your killer is still here. Close by. New Orleans and San Francisco were holiday excursions for her. My gut tells me that."

"It's visceral, eh?" Simmons shook some more pills into his hand and washed then down with bourbon. "Where can you pick up the trail now?"

"I don't know."

"If you don't know, then that leaves me in a quandary," Simmons confessed. "I can't retain you if we have no direction in our investigation together. Will the Department allow you to pursue this officially?"

Max thought about Quinnliven. "It seems unlikely at the moment."

"Well, then, why don't we do this? Christmas is next week and that's going to occupy everyone's time. I'll be on my vacation then. When I come back, we should sit down and discuss where things might lead us, down the road. Why don't we do that?"

☙

An hour later, Max wandered through the streets of the Playpen, half-drunk and carrying ten dollars in his jeans. He wanted to call Diana. Several times, he wrenched himself away from the gray tin phone booths.

"Calling back is for softies," he muttered aloud. Talking to himself eased his pain a bit. "Mushy stuff. I'm broke and scared, that's all. I know what'll happen."

Every cop knew what would happen. He would pick up another job, tending bar or driving an executive limousine. The Department would move slowly. His paperwork would clog down around coffee breaks, weekends, national holidays and the Christmas season.

Turning bitter, he would reach for liquor, either cool martinis in Playpen lounges or sweating six-packs from the corner superette.

Simmons was right, Max realized. They had done a lot of good work at finding Nancy/Charlene. Nobody else had even come close.

He realized he would never see Diana again. That seemed plain enough. He would not see her eyes crinkle up at her nonsense or feel her sweet weight.

Something about Simmons kept buzzing in Max's head. He wondered again what kind of father Simmons had been. Max could talk with Lily Sangster, the teacher, and then move onto Pruitt. He just might learn something.

So, he set his course for the school, trying to sober himself up.

## CHAPTER 35.

As he entered the school, he saw balloons and pink bunting hanging over the doorway. A long bed sheet in green pine and bright scarlet colors showed the words "Christmas Pageant Today" spraypainted across it. Drums and tambourines sounded downstairs. The same receptionist that Max remembered rose up to greet him.

"My name is Max Royster," he said. "I'd like to speak with Ms. Sangster."

"Ms. Sangster is downstairs with her class at the Christmas show," she said in her precise English accent. "So is everyone else. I'm in charge."

"I'm a police officer investigating Rusty Simmons death. Do you remember that I was here before with my boss, Sgt. Lipkin?"

"No, I don't recall that. I'm sorry. Do you have any identification?"

Max was caught flatfooted. "No, not now. I just need to speak with Ms. Sangster for a minute and then I'll be on my way."

"Unless this is an emergency of some kind, I can't interrupt the show to find her and bring her to you. The school had had some strange publicity because of the killings. Since you have no way of identifying yourself, I'm going to have to ask you to leave."

Max knew she could back up her words. A fast phone call to 911 would get him thrown out of his own high school.

"You may telephone her after five," she said. "This is our last day before Christmas vacation and we're very busy."

"It is kind of an emergency," Max said.

"What was the name again, sir?"

"Max Royster."

"Very well." She jotted it down. "If you don't leave now, Mr. Royster, I'll telephone the police."

A chubby schoolboy with rust-colored hair, wearing a school blazer came down the polished wooden hallway. He tried to pick his way silently past the receptionist.

"Brewster, what are you doing up here?" the receptionist asked. "Why aren't you downstairs at the play? They're about to start. Attendance is mandatory."

"Mr. McLaughlin sent me up to get his briefcase. He forgot it in the Common Room."

"See that you get downstairs in time for Mr. Pruitt's opening remarks," the receptionist said. "Mr. Royster, it's time to leave."

"Let me send a note down to Ms. Sangster," Max pleaded. "I know she'll come upstairs when she gets the note."

"I'll take the note," the schoolboy said. He wanted to read it. He always read other people's messages.

"Very well," the woman said. "But if she says she is too busy right now, you will leave. Is that understood?"

"Clearly," Max said. "If she says 'go', I'll go."

He scribbled out a message on a file card that the receptionist doled out.

> "I need to see you right away about the
> Simmons case. Very important.
> - Max Royster."

The schoolboy left with the note and the teacher's briefcase. Max sat and waited, tense and thirsty for some more cold white wine. It was going to be a long lean weekend for him without any money. Now would be a good time to rob a bank.

## CHAPTER 36.

The same schoolboy came back downstairs and handed the small file card back to the receptionist. She primly gave it to Max. The back of the card read:

"I can't talk with you now. Please call later.
- Lily Sangster"

"She doesn't wish to speak with you?" the receptionist said. "Then you'll have to leave, Mr. Royster."

The schoolboy hung in the doorway, intrigued by these adult doings.

Max stared at the note, stunned. The handwriting matched! It was the same as the grocery list. He snapped out his wallet with hands that were shaking and unfolded the photocopied shopping list that Nancy, the killer, had given to Jacky. This schoolteacher was Charlene and Nancy both. She was their killer.

"May I use your telephone?" Max asked. "It's an emergency."

"But it wasn't an emergency before? You said it was. No, Mr. Royster. You have to leave now."

"Give me the telephone."

He could get Emergency Services police units to cordon off the building and cover the service exits. Or else they would lose Charlene again.

"No!" She was finally losing her cool. "Didn't I make myself clear? No telephone. Please leave."

Max nodded and left the office, heading for the street door. She could not see him from the window now. He opened the street door just enough to let in the traffic noises from outside and then let it close again. He froze, feeling her listen for any other noise. Nothing stirred. Then he heard a file drawer open and the chair squeak.

ɤ

As he stole silently in his running shoes along the hallway, downstairs laughter covered Max's footsteps. He bent down low under the window so the receptionist could not see him.

Max came downstairs into a darkened auditorium where the whole school sat silently in rows. He waited to let his eyes adjust to the dark. His heart felt like a mustang horse breaking out against his chest.

"Gentlemen," Trumbull Pruitt said from the auditorium stage. "Each Christmas at St. Blaise's, it is our custom to present a series of low-budget theatrical spectaculars dealing with the Nativity in Bethlehem. This year, our breath is taken away by the interpretation of Christmas as seen from the viewpoint of Melchior, one of the Three Wise Men from the East who journeyed to Bethlehem. Crackling dialogue and sober scholarship combine to form this latest St. Blaise's original epic, put forward by Mr. Murtaugh's fourth grade."

The spotlight faded. Mr. Pruitt stepped down from in front of the curtain. Max strained his eyes again to see Lily.

A burgundy curtain rose. A small blond boy whose skin looked milky white under the spotlights stood on center stage, dressed in an Arab robe that dragged on the floor. He waved his small arm in a fanning gesture towards the audience.

"Hi, there," he said. "You remember me. I'm Melchior, one of the Three Wise Men. You read about me in the Bible."

A grownup stirred in the rear of the auditorium. Max squinted.

Lily Sangster bent down and whispered to some boys sitting on the floor. They got up and followed her to the doorway.

Lily kept moving the group. Max stepped towards her. They passed through the door.

"Don't shout and spook her," Max told himself. "The whole school will turn riot. And she'll wiggle free. Lock her in somewhere."

He stepped on hands, moving along the rows. Schoolboys squawked.

"Can I help you, sir?" one hefty teacher whispered, coming in front. Max did not know him.

"No, thanks."

"Are you a parent? This play is just for students and faculty."

"I'm leaving."

"Let me escort you out, sir. We've had some difficulty –"

Max shoved him aside and ran.

Lily had vanished with her group.

Max dashed through the same doorway.

Someone moved on the staircase above. Shoes creaked. A door opened then shut.

Max lunged up the stairs. His breathing sharpened.

His right hand dropped to his hip. But there was no Glock there anymore. He was running against a serial killer without a piece.

He came to the roof door. Someone's key hung in the lock. He pushed it open and stepped out onto the tar.

Lily sat on the parapet. The schoolboys grouped around her in their blue blazers. Saint Blaise emblems shining on their pockets. Lily held one schoolboy on her lap. Another leaned against her thigh.

She glared at Max, thirty feet away.

"We're story-telling here, Max," she said. " I excused my friends here from that drab play. Please leave us alone."

Her perfect teeth ground together.

"Miss Sangster, may I –"

"No talking, Mr. Royster. I knew that my time here was growing short. So I made ready to leave in a big way."

"I'm cold, Miss Sangster!" one of them whined. "Can we go inside?"

"Not yet, Cushing," she said. "Mr. Pruitt asked us to wait here."

"Guys," Max said. "Come away from the ledge."

"No, Mr. Royster," Lily said. "They're with me."

Max saw it. He stopped moving.

"Last night, I could feel my time growing short," Lily said. "With some new ID and a face change, I'll get another teaching job out West."

"What are you saying, Ms. Sangster?" one of them asked.

"You're out of time," Max said.

"What else do I have time for?" she asked. "So you can watch me escape. And live with your failure forever."

"Guys, come over here!" Max shouted. "Get away from the ledge."

"Who're you?" one asked.

"He's a psycho!" Lily said. "Child molester. Protect me, boys."

Max ran forward. Lily tossed the boy on her lap over the edge.

"AHHHHHH!" he screamed, pinwheeling. His blond hair fluttered. The eyes bugged. She let him fall.

The others skittered. Lily grabbed another by his throat. She lifted him to her hip.

"No closer! No closer, you!" she spat at Max. "I'll toss each one of them off! You back off me!"

Max stopped. He felt sick. The boys stayed huddled near Lily. She spun and flung the boy at Max, using all her strength. Max leaped back. The boy landed heavily on the tar roof.

Lily was moving, going down the fire escape alongside the building. Some of the boys tried to follow her.

"No! No!" Max shouted. "You guys, come on! Come on over here."

They milled around in confusion. They were dangerously near the edge.

"She shouldn't have brought us up here," one said.

"That's right," Max said. "So, please. Go back inside. Tell Mr. Pruitt what happened. Go find him."

"Let's go," the boy agreed. "Back inside before they catch us here."

They all rushed to the door and down the staircase, shouting and weeping over their dead classmate.

Max swung onto the fire escape and saw Lily clambering below. He went down the fire escape after her. She was almost to the ground now.

He looked but there was nobody at any of the windows.

Nobody to get him help. He raced down the metal steps. She was at the sliding ladder part now. She released the catch and the fifteen-foot ladder started going down to the ground. But she whirled around, shrieking.

Something was caught. The ladder had snagged the sleeve of her loose dress and caught it in the sliding mechanism. Lily was trapped. The ladder stopped, eight feet above the sidewalk.

Max saw this. Passing the third story, Lily tugged and screamed. Her glasses flew off and cracked on the sidewalk below. The fallen schoolboy lay moaning and writhing. Blood spattered around him.

Lily tore her dress and pulled free of the ladder. Max was twelve feet from her. She slid down the ladder, hung by both hands and dropped to the sidewalk. On flat ground, she could outrun him. They both knew it.

Lily started running. Max was still coming down the fire escape. He swung furiously over the side, gripped the rail with both hands and dropped twelve feet down to the pavement. His feet stung him.

Now she was running down the service alleyway behind the school. She turned and ran up to the East End Avenue, heading west. Max saw other faces in the school windows now.

Somebody would telephone. But the radio cars would not be able to find him if Lily kept running. She would move too fast.

Traffic parted as Lily ran across the avenue. Max was at least forty feet behind her and he was no runner. But he wore sneakers.

Lily had flat dress shoes. He could hear them smacking against the sidewalk.

They were already at Lexington Avenue. Max had no idea they had gone so far. But he was not quitting. He slammed a man's arm while the man was talking on the pay phone. The man's face turned up, angry.

"Police! Call 911!" Max shouted as he went past. "911! I need help!"

Lily was flashing across the Park Avenue divider now, sprinting through the strip of grass and shrubs. Max came up, coughing and hacking. Then he saw a blue-and-white car coming up the avenue. But they were too far away. If he went to get them, he would lose Lily. She would turn into a service doorway or crouch down between cars. Then she would be gone.

Max waved his arms, hoping they would see him. The car turned a corner and was gone.

Traffic on Madison Avenue blocked Lily. The light was against her. She danced on one foot and then on another, looking back at Max.

The wall of trucks hemmed her in. She ran downtown on Madison. Max reached the comer. She was gone. There was no sign of the gray dress. He could not stand upright. Wheezing bent him double. Lily was gone.

He scanned the double-parked cars and vans. Shoppers went by on the sidewalk. Horns sounded. A hatchback went by with the ghetto blaster boom box radio beating against the air. Then he saw something move. Lily ran across Madison Avenue from where she had been hiding behind a truck. Max flung himself after her again.

Then they were at Fifth Avenue and the entrance to Central Park. Max followed her along the stone path, gaining on her. He was twenty feet in back now. They had not been this close before.

She ran past the Alice-in-Wonderland bronze statue. Mothers with their children looked at her flying past. Then she gained the knoll, ran through bikers and joggers on the roadway and past the Boathouse on the lake.

Max saw that she was heading into the tree groves. She could ambush him there or lose him easily.

She turned and saw the cop still chasing her. Then she was in the park. She felt her power come back strongly. She soared like an eagle up the granite rocks along the lake, drawing Max in deeper and deeper. They were far away from the roadway now, along the boat lake. Max lost sight of her but kept moving furiously.

Suddenly, she struck him without warning, coming from his blind side. Her arms snaked around his throat. She had him tightly before he could stop running. He fell heavily, exhausted. Lily was fresh and growing stronger. She worked her way behind him. All men were soft here. Their muscles were useless. Nothing protected them. She could penetrate them.

She had just stopped, hidden herself and waited for him to go past.

Max pried at her arm with his panicked fingers. She was bearing down. His neck bones grated. He was starting to black out.

"Die," she whispered, her lips very close to his ear. "Die, my Saint Blaise's cop. You all used me. My father did, too. All you rich boys used me like a whore. Die now."

Max reared up and tried to shake her but she was too strong. His thick fingers reached up to yank her hair, but it was too far away. His throat was in the crook of her arm. He was on the ground with her straddling him. His face was pressed against the dirt.

His arms flailed in Lily's death grip. He screamed. She bore him down with all her weight. He got his palm flat against the ground and pushed to one side. She held on. He rocked his body and tried again. This time, he rolled to the side with her still choking him. Strong arms tight around his throat. He thrashed and cursed and roared, and they were rolling down the slope together, one body on top of the other, rolling down until he felt the lake water on his face.

Lily groped for a tighter grip, for the final twist. Max rolled deeper into the water with her still strangling him.

She tried to keep him on the shore. He went deeper. They hit a sunken rock. Lily screamed as her elbow smashed against it. Her arm went numb.

Max slithered and broke free. Her hand smashed against his throat in a karate strike. He gagged once. They were standing now in water up to their waists. Lily tried to kick but the water stopped her leg. Max flung an arm around her neck from the front, spun her around and threw his own body out flat behind her.

Exhausted, he used his own body weight for power. She weakened and choked. Max dug along the bottom of the pond with his free hand, scooped up a jagged rock and smashed it twice against Lily's wet head. Blood showed. She fought back. Max slammed her with his forearm against her throat, and she fell backwards towards the shore. She pulled herself along the ground, trying to get to her feet.

Max came out of the water and grabbed her ankle. He flipped her over onto her back and pounded the rock against her left kneecap. The knee broke. Lily howled, trying to drag the useless leg away. Max smashed her other knee with the rock, crippling her. She tried to get to her feet but the smashed knees gave way, and she fell back down helplessly.

She could not get away.

Finally, Max saw the familiar blue-and-white car coming through the trees thirty feet away, lights spinning in their sockets, showing red-orange, red-orange. Other cars were streaking behind. Max could not move any more. He lay stretched along the shore and cried, panting brokenly. He hoped that sleep would come and take him.

# CHAPTER 37.

"How could Lily travel like she did?" Diana asked, leaning over Max on his day bed. Outside, the sun was setting and sending colored rivulets through the concrete edges of the city.

"Saved her money," Max said. "The passion for murder was important to her. Nobody really checks references when you're willing to work cheap. In the sexual underground, where she grew up, re-papering your own life is easy. I'd like to learn her secrets myself."

Diana looked at the angry purple-and-strawberry bruises around Max's neck and shivered a little.

"What will happen to her?" she asked.

"Her assigned counsel will dance a hopscotch fandango. Try to convince the court she is insane. The Manhattan DA will cha-cha-cha back with evidence of her rational mind. My money says that she'll pass upstate to some locked-down home for the bewildered. Probably lift weights a lot. Read and masturbate. Run eight miles a night in her room."

"Simmons won't do much better, feeling guilty about sleeping with his son's killer."

"Cash softens the blow," Max snorted. "Like the Chinese say, he who has money can eat sherbet in hell. He'll take a cruise, obtain expensive therapy and console himself with some other young women. He'll continue on. So will the Playpen. You watch it happen."

"The Department's taking you back. They have to. And a grateful America will reward Max Royster," Diana smirked impudently.

"Happens only in movies. That lawyer Decker is still suing me for denting his client. Get ready for the pain. The blue bloods running the Playpen can relax about their sons and heirs playing lacrosse in Central Park now. Nobody remembers how the threat ended. They'll want no further trouble along those lines."

Max blew out a long, weary breath, the bones in his bruised shoulders and neck creaking.

"And the next boring Playpen cocktail party that you're at," Max went on, "with nothing more to chat about, you'll look around at the stuffy white-haired executives in the rich dark suits, settled back in comfortable leather armchairs, with their slim trophy wives patiently alongside. Scent of Scotch-and-water and discreet perfume. Rich cigars from the balcony. Please remember tonight."

"I'll remember that Max Royster risked everything to keep their sons alive," Diana said.

"I hope they remember, too," Max said. "Let me come around and be their doorman."

They kissed.

# SPECIAL THANKS

To Persia Walker, novelist, for her untiring help and suggestions.

To Detective-Investigators Mark Baldessare and Fareed "Fred" Ghussin and all the other cops and federal agents who taught me so much about hunting our real-life serial killers.

To the ***Spy, the Movie*** team – Jim MacPherson, Alex Klymko, Charles Messina and all the rest of the gang for a grand adventure in screenwriting.

To Nad Wolinska, for her excellently creepy cover.

To my writing partner, Lynwood Shiva Sawyer, for his support and encouragement over the years

And my thanks to that wonderful woman, companion and friend from Guangzhou, China, who shares my adventures and my life.

CPSIA information can be obtained at www.ICGtesting.com
Printed in the USA
BVOW042119050212
282143BV00001B/1/P

9 780984 881000